The Daiquiri Girls

the

daiquiri

girls

Toni Graham

University of

Massachusetts Press

Amherst

for my parents,
Joseph and Maxine Johnson Avila

This book is the winner of the Associated Writing Programs 1997
Award in Short Fiction. AWP is a national, nonprofit organization
dedicated to serving American letters, writers, and programs
of writing. AWP's headquarters are at George Mason
University, Fairfax, Virginia.

Copyright © 1998 by Toni Graham
Printed in the United States of America
LC 98-35813
ISBN 1-55849-167-8
Designed by Kristina Kachele
Set in Galliard with Emigre Matrix Script Regular display
by Keystone Typesetting, Inc.
Printed and bound by BookCrafters
Library of Congress Cataloging-in-Publication Data
Graham, Toni, date
The daiquiri girls / Toni Graham.
p.   cm.
"Winner of the Associated Writing Program's 1997
Award in Short Fiction"—T. p. verso.
ISBN 1-55849-167-8 (alk. paper)
1. United States—Social life and customs—20th century—Fiction.
2. City and town life—United States—Fiction.
3. Women—United States—Fiction. I. Title.
PS3557.R2234D35   1998
813'.54—dc21   98-35813
CIP

British Library Cataloguing in Publication data are available.

Forgetting is as important as remembering.

—WILLIAM JAMES

Acknowledgments

Many of the chapters originally appeared in the following journals.

Ascent 18, no. 2 (Fall 1993): "Microslips"
American Fiction, no. 2 (1988): "Jump!"
Chiron Review, no. 51 (Summer 1997): "Lying in Bed"
Clockwatch Review, 1998: "Kilter"
Five Fingers Review, no. 5: "Shadow Boxing"
Mississippi Mud, no. 38 (1996): "My Higher Power"
Mississippi Review 19, no. 1-2 (Fall 1990): "Tooth and Nail"
Nob Hill Gazette (San Francisco), June 1987 "Cinema Verite"
Playgirl: January 1985, "Endings"; October 1986, "In Season" (as "Pursuit"); October 1988, "Faithful"
Short Story Review (Winter 1985): "Skin and Bone"
Worcester Review 17, no. 1-2 (1996): "Reunion"
Writers' Forum, no. 24 (Fall 1998): "Blood Bank"
"Faithful" also appeared in *Zipzap* e-zine, no. 2 (Summer 1995), the Internet, World Wide Web, and "Endings" appeared in a slightly different version in *Santa Clara Review* 85, no. 3 (Winter 1998).

I wish to extend my gratitude to:

Salvatore Zeno, for being my anchor.
My writing group, for their brilliance, editing, friendship and moral support: Nona Caspers, Margi Dunlap, Shelley Gage, Hillary Illick, Ellen Thompson and Barbara Tomash.

Robert Boswell and Brian Bouldrey.

My many teachers and mentors, including Paul Bailiff, Michelle Carter, David Field, Molly Giles, Leo Litwak, the late Bert Miller, Gus Pagels, the late Sara Vogan, and William Wiegand.

And of course the Associated Writing Programs and the University of Massachusetts Press.

contents

jane

kilter

"Cato! Bad dog!" screams the neighbor with the crew cut and the handlebar mustache as he tries to break up the snarling fight between his dog and the tattooed woman's dog. "Artemis! Artemis!" Jane hears the woman shout, and when the dogs finally stop growling and yipping, she hears the two masters apologize to each other.

It used to be that she woke to the sound of her husband's breathing, or to the sound of Betsy watching cartoons in the other room. Later, she awoke with Andrew, and then with Lars. Now Jane wakes to the sound of the dogs out in the street. Her neighborhood has gone gay, which is just as well with her, since they all keep their gardens looking good and no one appears to wish to rape her. The gays have no children and while some of the lesbians have been inseminated and push strollers together with their babies, most of them have dogs instead of kids.

Her daughter, Betsy, lives with her boyfriend now; Bert lives with his third wife; Andrew lives with his second wife; and Jane lives with no one. This would have seemed hideous to her at one time, but now she almost accepts it with a shrug and feels a certain detachment from her own life. She thinks of the men she once loved as "The Father, the Son, and the Holy Ghost." She had married Bert because he was like her father; Andrew had married her because she was like his mother; and then there had been Lars, the Holy Ghost, dead from a New Year's Eve crash on Doyle Drive, his death a complete cliché—one more drunk driver crashing and burning on the ever-dangerous approach to the Bridge.

Because Jane and Lars were not married, Lars's family had been in charge of his funeral, pushing her off to one side, a widow not entitled to wear weeds. There was a certain amount of bitterness, since Lars died alone in the car after a quarrel with Jane at a New Year's party and they all said he would still be alive if it weren't for her, that essentially she had killed him. She suspected she was nearly barred from the funeral, but in any case, she sat alone in the back of the chapel so she did not have to see his body. Like pagans, they had laid her dead lover out in a grotesque open casket reeking of orchids. He had been decapitated in the Miata's crash and there had been whispers amongst the older funeral-goers, some of Lars's southern California friends, about how reminiscent it was of Jayne Mansfield's death — the convertible, the white-blonde hair on the hood of the car and the torso still at the wheel. She knew better, though, because Jayne Mansfield had been wearing a wig — her body went one way, her head another, the wig off in still another direction. Lars had a full head of almost silver-blond hair; he was proud of no baldness or gray hair at forty. The family paid an astronomical sum for a special make-up man flown in from Beverly Hills to reunite Lars with his argentine head and to hide all the gashes and seams. She heard Lars's sister say that the make-up artist was the same one who did Elvis — the guy who had seen to it that Elvis was buried with one side of his upper lip curled up in his customary sneer.

Her sex drive never came back after the funeral; it has been three years now. She had what her doctor called "ovarian failure" not long after they buried Lars, so the reason for her lack of libido is unclear — it could be grief or just old age.

"Bad, bad, bad, bad, BAD!" screams Cato's master. She wonders why the man does not take the dog to obedience school instead of pretending every morning to be shocked at the misbehavior of his untrained canine.

Shall I get out of bed? she thinks. Or shall I just lie here? Shall I go catatonic, blow my brains out, go to work? The wheel stops on "go to work," because she knows she ought to and because Betsy is expecting to meet her for lunch that day, and if a daughter cannot count on her mother, what is there left in this world? Catatonia would have been first choice, however. She remembers the night a few months before Lars was killed, the night he decided to check his answering machine before he came to bed. She was already waiting in the bed, excited, champagne and lust in her veins as Lars brushed his teeth and turned out all the lights before they retired. It was Lars's fortieth birthday and they had dined out on oysters and champagne and she was primed for the birthday fuck, had been dying for it since the instant his hand slid under the hem of her dress in the restaurant.

She heard him dialing the phone in the hall and asked, "Who are you calling?" Why was he making a telephone call after midnight, naked on the way to her bed? She impulsively reached for her eyeglasses from the nightstand, knowing that for some reason she could always hear better when she wore the glasses. Their underwear and the champagne flutes and some lavender tissue paper from the gifts were scattered around the bedroom floor. Lars's black Calvin briefs had randomly landed on her pink lace bikinis and this excited her even more. He mumbled that he just wanted to see if he had any messages at his apartment, and this touched her, because it made him seem like a small boy, wanting to know if he had any special birthday calls while they were out.

The woman's voice was so loud that Jane could hear it from ten feet away as it came through the telephone receiver. "Hello Lars — it's Kimberlee," she heard the woman say, her voice all false-throatiness. "Just wanted to wish you a happy birthday," she said. "Let's get together soon, ya hear?" She sounded the way Jane imagined a telephone-sex woman would sound, the voice full of entendre. Lars put the receiver down and came into the bedroom with the poker face she was glad to have had her glasses on to see. He said his mother had called to wish him a happy birthday.

She had felt herself fly apart, but not in a herky-jerky disjointed way.

She had felt like a ball of rubber bands that snapped but then reverberated, oscillating, and she had just let her arms and legs and neck go limp like strands of India rubber and felt her eyelids rest at half-mast, so that she saw nothing except the lavender tissue paper out of the corner of an eye. She didn't even remember getting under the bed.

"You mean, under the covers," her daughter corrected her when she tried to tell her about it.

"No, I guess I got under the bed when I went catatonic, or just before, because I remember Lars pulling me out from under there by one ankle. He was yelling, 'Can you hear me? What's wrong? Can you hear my voice?' and of course I *could* hear him, but I just couldn't move or talk."

"Do you always have to overreact?" Betsy had asked. "I mean, intense is interesting, but deranged isn't."

Instead of telling Lars what she had overheard, she kept silent, blaming her attack on an allergic reaction to the oysters.

Now she is exhausted from lack of sleep. The smoke alarm in the hallway had begun beeping in the middle of the night as a warning that the battery was low. She had not been up to getting out of bed at three in the morning and climbing on a ladder, so she had tried to ignore it, but the noise had awakened her at regular intervals. She tries to summon the energy to raise her head from the pillow and begin to get ready for work. She is assistant to the CEO of a national industrial supply company, but the job is not what it used to be. Mr. Huggins, the seventy-five-year-old senior patriarch in a family business that never went public, has become dotty and is half blind from an inoperable retinal problem. Huggins still comes to the office every day, and the family still want him to be known as the head of the firm, but he's been nothing but a figurehead for a number of years. His coherence went before his vision and everyone in his life is committed to pretending he still possesses both. Jane commands a decent salary, but she does little except read things to Huggins or field phone calls for him so that no one can figure out he's gaga. She goes in on Saturdays occasionally to get the lay of the land when Huggins isn't there —

to look through his desk drawers to see that he has not hidden any important documents or left a half-eaten pastrami sandwich to molder or draw rodents. She has found pornographic magazines, valuable stock certificates, and fetid cheese Danish crammed into his desk drawers.

The morning goes more quickly than she had expected. Huggins is cutting out articles from the large-print edition of the *Wall Street Journal* with a pair of scissors, like a little kid with paper dolls. "Would you mind making half a dozen copies of this article about what that imbecile in the White House wants to do about the situation overseas?" he asks Jane. His voice is remarkably vibrant for a man his age, but he has developed an annoying habit of clearing his throat after every two or three words. She finds herself waiting for him to do it, gritting her teeth as he speaks, waiting for each regular "Harrumph!"

"I want to — harrumph, hooh — send a copy to Decker and to Soames and to — hoomph, hrummp — MacAlindon," he says.

When he hands her the first page of the article to copy, she sees that he has inadvertently hacked off the last paragraph. "Whoops, Mister H., something's a bit off kilter, here," she says, looking through the wastebasket to see if the portion he cut off ended up there.

"You're using that word incorrectly," he says, cutting away with the orange-handled shears from the Office Club.

"Which word?"

"Kilter," he tells her.

"I beg your pardon?"

"Kilter," he says, "is a little *Jewish* fish."

"Thank you," she says, feeling her face flame. She wonders if he means gefilte fish, then envisions kippers with yarmulkes, and for an instant she imagines the orange plastic handles of the scissors protruding from the old man's back. She leaves the room to copy the foreign policy article and does not mention to him that the last paragraph is missing.

She takes the underground streetcar from the office to the theater district to meet her daughter for lunch. When she comes up to street level on the escalator, she sees them all there, the usual bums who sit or stand in the very same spots every day, though they are not called bums anymore. She suspects that the ones with Evian bottles are drinking gin, the ones with Snapple bottles are drinking red wine, the ones with Sprite bottles are drinking white wine, and the ones with Martinelli apple juice bottles are drinking whiskey. Some of them carry only cups for money or signs professing hunger. They all smoke cigarettes, though she knows they cost nearly three dollars a pack these days. She gives two quarters to her regular guy, the one she has chosen to give to because he seems mentally ill — unable to work as she sees it — and because he often says to her, "Thank you, my darling."

There is a sandwich board propped up in front of the espresso-to-go window, reading "Great espresso, fresh pastries, bad advice," and she begins to smile, but then she notices a man asleep on the sidewalk near his wheelchair. He is lying on his back with his feet flat on the ground and his knees bent tent-style in the air as he sleeps and she wonders why he needs a wheelchair. She has a hideous surge of emotion as she slaloms through the various panhandlers on the sidewalk. She is torn right down the middle between the impulse to sob with pity and the urge to kick out at them as viciously as she can. She is all too aware that if Huggins dies, she could end up on the sidewalk herself. She knows she is not mentioned in Huggins's will and that she will be given severance pay and shown the door as soon as he croaks. She has made no contingency plans and has been too despondent since Lars's death to do anything other than drag herself into the office each day, with absolutely no thought of even the next day to come.

She walks by one of the larger, more glamorous department stores and looks at the window displays, happy to focus on fantasy. There is a glitzy tableau in the corner windows, all designer western wear: four-hundred-dollar cowboy boots on beautiful mannequins, dolls that look as anorexic as real models. There is denim and there are sequins and beribboned ten-gallon hats, and a mannequin with fake cleavage who appears to be twirling a lasso. Music from Rodgers and Hammerstein's *Oklahoma* blares from loudspeakers, manic and joyful. The music is sheer euphoria, auditory dope. "O! What a Beautiful Morning!" and more of the same. She remembers watching Hollywood musicals as a girl, carried away with the bliss and the promise of life, with the exalted human spirit.

What if I'd found out the truth then? she muses. What if my mother or a fortune teller or a disclaimer after one of those musicals had spelled out the truth: You won't live happily ever after; there aren't seven brides for seven brothers. All you'll do is work; you won't lounge on the Riviera or stroll on the Via Veneto. Why hadn't someone had the kindness to warn her, Hey Janie-girl, guess what: Those people wearing the T-shirts printed "Life's a Bitch and Then You Die" are absolutely correct — that's the real Dead Sea scroll.

She curses the fact that she is allergic to Prozac, which she discovered shortly after Lars's funeral. In the past, there had at least been champagne or martinis or blood-and-thunder sex with Lars to take the edge off of things, but now the misery is relentless. Alcohol just gives her hot flashes and headaches, and since Lars died, the only man to enter her bedroom has been a prowler. The burglar rifled her bureau drawers at three in the morning while she lay trembling, pretending to be asleep, then crept off with the diamond earrings she had left on top of the bureau.

Where are the endorphins supposed to come from? she wonders. Is she supposed to take up jogging like the morons she sees everywhere running around the city together or alone, sweat pouring off them, headphones over their ears, spaced-out smiles or ugly grimaces on their faces?

"No, thank you," she says to the man selling the *Street Sheet* newspaper, and again to the young woman handing out Scientology leaflets posing the question, "Did Your Problems Begin Before You Were Born?" and to the derelict who asks, "How bout a little dime, Slim?" and to the man, deaf or pretending to be deaf, who is trying to thrust sign-language cards upon her. "No, no, no thank you, no." No, not at all, uh-uhh, negative, negatory.

Betsy is already seated, reading the *Times* at a window table, sipping a glass of white wine. She looks exactly like her father, Jane's ex-husband, and like her half-sister, a product of Bert's first marriage, and also like her young half-brother, the offspring from Bert's third marriage. It is as if Bert cloned himself three times, in male and female versions, his three wives functioning as little more than hatcheries for his progeny, seemingly contributing no genes of their own. Betsy looks up and says, "Hello, Mother," with Bert's smile, her hair in a ponytail the way Bert's was when she met him.

"Am I late?" she asks her daughter as she sits down, knowing she is not. Betsy is early for everything, was even born a week early, before Jane had thought to pack her bag for the hospital. She is a compulsive girl, always prepared. Jane had been shocked to learn when she stayed with her and Stu one weekend that before she went to bed at night Betsy set the table for breakfast and even put the coffee beans into the grinder. She placed her little bedroom slippers right by the side of the bed so that her bare feet never touched the ground.

Betsy glances at her watch and says, "You're right on time. I came a few minutes early; I wanted to read the paper." She lowers her voice. "Don't look now, but I want you to sneak a look at that man sitting at the bar."

Jane takes care not to turn her head, but ventures a look at the man on a bar stool, knowing her dark glasses hide her eyes. "The guy with the long stringy hair?" she asks, sotto voce. The man is sipping a cocktail and chatting with the person on the stool next to him.

"Yes. Does he look familiar to you?" she asks.

Jane looks again, but he does not remind her of anyone in particular. "What about him?" she asks her daughter.

"He fits the description, exactly, of the serial killer who's been terrorizing the Bay Area," Betsy says. "I saw a flyer on the way over, and I remember seeing something about it in the *Examiner* last week."

How odd, she thinks, that Betsy would think that a murderer on the loose would just happen to be sitting in the restaurant where we're lunching. She wants to suggest that maybe her daughter has been watching too much "America's Most Wanted," but she restrains herself. She suspects that it is simply the man's shoulder-length hair that has made him a suspect in her daughter's mind. She takes after Bert, whose bohemian days are long behind him now that he is an investment banker — what Lou Reed used to call a "suit-and-tie-John." Betsy's boyfriend is one of those sixteen-hour-a-day software mavens that one meets everywhere these days, and Jane thinks it is no wonder that Betsy is so tense all the time.

"He's drinking manhattans," Betsy hisses. "When I got here, I noticed the bartender take away two empty manhattan glasses and he made the guy a third drink, and it wasn't even noon."

"Well, good for him," she says. "I'm sure I'd do the same thing if I could get away with it." She knows that Betsy is oblivious to the implications of having ordered white wine before noon, and she knows that when Betsy belts down several more glasses at lunch and at dinner and alone at home while she waits for Stu to get home from Silicon Valley, she will not consider this to be anything like the man with the manhattans.

"What about the flyer about the serial killer?" she asks her daughter. "How exactly was he described?" She watches the man closely as Betsy answers.

"Long, stringy, dirty-looking hair," she says, "Gaunt, pale, and hollow cheeked. In other words, exactly like this guy."

"Exactly like every junkie in town," she says, laughing. "And like half the alcoholics, and maybe like this poor Joe at the bar, who by the way has a very nice smile and is talking quite amiably with the guy next to him. He looks a bit sickly, maybe, but not like a maniac or a pervert."

Betsy shakes her head in disapproval, saying nothing.

"Really, Betz, he seems to be charming the person he's talking to —

they're chuckling. I don't think he's the Bay Area serial killer, hollow cheeks or no."

Betsy scowls like an old lady and shoots a look at the man.

Oh, poor Betz, she thinks — she's uptight as she can be. Young Stu has made a matron out of her and they're not even married yet. At the thought of the wedding she knows will come, of having to put up with the whole damned circus Stu's Boston Brahmin parents will want, she feels a roiling in her stomach. At the same time, she finds herself envying her daughter: Betsy is a pinched-up old bag in the body of a lovely young woman; I'm a wild woman in the body of a middle-aged third-rater. The truth is she was better looking than Betsy when she was her age, but as for now, she would be lucky to have Betsy's bland good looks.

"Get the waiter, would you Sweetie? I'd like to have a daiquiri," she says. She hopes the drink does not make her break out in the embarrassing flush and sweat that alcohol and caffeine have begun to bring down on her. She thinks as she waits for the drink: I've been bad, good, happy, sad, well off, and broke. But I was *always* young. When did I get old? If I had Betsy's fresh face and tight body, I wouldn't pin myself down with a jerk like Stu Williams, and I wouldn't have lunch with my mother, and I wouldn't sit around reading the *Times* and grumbling about serial killers on the loose. I'd find someone just like Lars — I don't care that he was a liar and a bit of a scoundrel! I would find another Lars and I would tell Huggins to go to hell in a handbasket, and I would fly to Cancun tomorrow and drink champagne until dawn and I would fuck my brains out. Yes, I would.

"Stu and I have started running," Betsy says, looking as if she expects her mother to congratulate her.

"I'm surprised you two can find time," she answers, "especially with Stu's schedule." She is certain she has withheld any trace of irony from her tone.

"We get up at 4:30," Betsy announces. "I thought I was starting to get a little cellulite, and Stu was getting a spare tire, so we started getting up an hour earlier to run."

Her daughter has a golden tan, adorable fluffy blonde hair on her slim, freckled arms, and she knows the cellulite is more notion than reality. Her eyes are a devastating blue, crystalline as pub-ice, fringed with naturally black lashes. Her face is not Garbo, not even Basinger, but it is infinitely angelic and free of lines and age spots. When they leave the restaurant together, any man on the street will stare at Betsy and look through Jane as if she is invisible. Worse: not worth a glance, a superfluous old duenna. It seems like only last week that she was walking down the street with Betsy in a baby stroller: Betz a drooling, bald lump; Jane fending off unwanted advances even with a baby in tow. And it was in fact only four short years ago when Lars took her to Puerto Vallarta and she'd still been able to walk proudly on the beach in a jade green string-bikini that Lars swore matched her eyes, and she'd made Lars shout and weep in bed in their hotel room half the night.

She would have jumped into the coffin with Lars like the women in India do, had she known what was in store for her, known that only three years down the line she would find herself relegated to membership in the unofficial league of hags, the invisible crew of over-the-hill women with ovarian failure and bifocals, taking calcium and estrogen and Centrum Silver every morning and forgetting what it feels like to have a man's hand on their breasts. This is all a mistake! she feels like screaming out. I'm a man killer, a Jezebel, death-in-bed. But she knows she is not one bit different from some sadsack fifty-year-old bald guy who still thinks of himself as a stud with a full head of luxuriant curls and fancies himself a bushy-haired Romeo.

She feels as if she is trapped inside someone else's body, the way transsexuals claim to feel. She had felt this way as an adolescent, too. At twelve or thirteen, she had perceived herself as an exciting, sensual woman, but she had still inhabited the body of a child. She had felt like Brigitte Bardot, a sex kitten, a temptress, but when she looked into the mirror she would be shocked to see someone who looked more like Shirley Temple, a child with chapped legs she was not yet allowed to shave and with the pathetic breast buds of puberty. It is happening again, because now she feels like a vamp in her prime, but when she looks into a mirror she sees someone like her mother, a woman with a puffy face and a slack jaw, with hair that is obviously tinted. She realizes: You go through the same things on the way out as you did on the way up. Huggins is now in his second childhood: a pitiful bald baby, unable to function without help. She is in her second adolescence, hormones on the blink. She is Mata Hari on the inside, an ugly duckling on the outside. But this time, she will not turn into a swan.

"He's leaving," Betsy says.

Jane snaps out of her reverie, seeing that she has nearly killed the daiquiri and that Betsy has been picking at a shrimp and endive salad. In front of her is a Niçoise salad she does not remember ordering. She looks over at the bar and explodes into laughter, having to clap her hand over her mouth so as not to make a scene. She feels the sting of a bit of rum coming up through her nose as she laughs while drinking. She knows Betsy will be revolted and embarrassed if she sees booze flying from her mother's nose, so she tries to get a grip on herself. But the "serial killer" at the bar has gingerly lowered himself from the bar stool, saying a word or two to the person he's been conversing with, and has started slowly toward the door, picking his way forward with a cane.

"Your serial killer is a blind man," she tells her daughter.

Betsy jerks her head around to stare at the man with the shoulder-length hair as he taps his way out with a red-tipped cane that is as slim and as white as a cigarette. She sees that Betsy is irritated to have been wrong. Jane is disgusted with herself for feeling so thrilled to be able to say I-told-you-so, and in fact, she does not say it. She says instead, "Is there anything in the *Times* about that woman in Sweden? The dead old lady?"

Betsy shakes her head. "What old lady?"

"She was dead for two years before anyone noticed," she says. "Not one person realized the old gal was dead in her bed. Her pension checks went directly into her bank account and her bills were paid automatically via computer every month. No one even noticed she was gone."

"Stop feeling sorry for yourself, Mother," Betsy says, her mild tone devoid of the canny brutality in her words.

She telephones Huggins from a pay phone after lunch, but he is still lunching at the Pacific Union Club and she gets the answering machine with her own voice on it. She listens to her taped self say in a smooth voice full of false efficiency that Mr. Huggins is out of the office but that one of his staff will be happy to call you back immediately if you will leave your name and number and state the purpose of your call. It is as big a lie as everything else. She is his staff and she is not going to telephone anyone in the world for Huggins today. She leaves a message: "Mr. Huggins, I neglected to tell you that I have a doctor's appointment and won't be back this afternoon. Don't forget that when you get back from the P.U. Club, the barber will be coming up for your trim. I left a check for him under the paperweight on your desk; it's in a red envelope." She has begun buying red envelopes and thick red felt pens for the office so that Huggins can see them. She has to leave notes for him on bright yellow stick-on sheets, since he would never notice a piece of plain white paper.

At the thought of the bus ride home, she suddenly feels drained and shaky so she hails a cab. She had ignored Betsy's barb and changed the subject and the luncheon had concluded on a pleasant note, but her hands had begun to tremble and she had pretended to have no appetite so that her daughter would not see her hands shaking as she ate. The cabby is listening to Rush Limbaugh on the radio and does not speak a word as he drives her home. She thinks he might be sulking because he wanted an airport fare and discovered she is going only a couple of miles. The back of his neck is smooth and elegant, and his hair is the same cold blond as Lars's had been. Oh Christ, not Lars again, she thinks. She is a pragmatist: She knows that if she found another man, this ceaseless yearning for Lars, the twisted obsession with him would stop. The only cure for a broken heart is a new lover, she'd found that out very early on. She does not kid herself; she loves Lars because there is no one else to love, no one alive that she can cling to. She is weary of carrying a dead man on her back.

Rush is bitching about the First Lady and the cabby has turned up the volume as if he is hanging on every word, or as if he wants Jane to hear it too.

"Right here," she tells him as he turns on to her street, and pulls out her purse. For some crazy reason, it comes into her mind that Freudians believe that a purse is a symbol for the female genitalia, the way a necktie is a symbol for the male's. She feels embarrassed as he watches her fumble in the purse for money, and the embarrassment becomes profound when she discovers she has no cash.

"Oh my gosh, I didn't realize I just spent the last of the cash I had on lunch," she says. "You'll have to forgive me, and I'll give you a check for it."

"GET OUT!" he says, reaching into the back seat and flinging the door open wide.

She is stunned, nearly speechless, and actually stutters as she asks him, "What? Do you mean you don't want to take a check? Why not? — I've given drivers checks before."

"Just get out, lady," he says. "I have no means to cash checks."

"You mean, you don't have a bank account?" she blurts out, dumbfounded.

"Is that any of your business?" he shouts. "You think I want to be bothered with you and your checks for a small-potatoes short-hop fare like this. You're not worth the trouble, lady. Get out — you're holding me up."

She feels as if some gigantic plug has been pulled from her and that a vortex is sucking her down like water through an unstoppered drain. "I am not a bum," she says in a shrill voice, and she feels the urge to laugh at herself for sounding like Nixon's I-am-not-a-crook speech. But things grow worse in that very same instant, and she segues from being Richard Nixon to being Billy Graham. She hears herself say in a ferocious voice, "You'll go to hell for this — God will punish you." She believes neither in hell nor in God nor in herself and has no idea why she has said this. She sees that the cabby is afraid of her now, that he thinks she is insane. She slams the car door shut behind her and he burns rubber peeling out.

She walks up the stairs to her apartment holding her purse clutched in front of her with both hands and has a flash of remembrance of Betsy learning to walk. The baby was slow to start walking, nearly nineteen months, and Bert had been voicing his concerns, suggesting they "have her evaluated." Jane's great-aunt Alicia had given Betsy a little stuffed bunny at Easter, an ugly thing, really, with a painted-on leer and disturbingly stiff ears that stood straight up in the air. The thing wore a cheap polyester jump suit that was sewn on to it and which smelled vaguely like petroleum. "Luvee-Bunnee" was embroidered over the pocket of the jump suit like the name of a gas station attendant. She and Bert had wanted to ditch the animal, but Betsy had been crazy about it and had renamed it "Lucky," which had inexplicably wrenched at Jane's heart. Betz had been crawling around a fews days after Easter when suddenly she rose to a stand, holding Lucky in front of her like a steering wheel. She had taken a couple of steps, and before Jane could even exclaim over it, little Betsy had actually gone from a walk to a run, had gone on a tear all over the house, running barefoot and bowlegged, shrieking with delight as she discovered she was upright and mobile. From then on, whenever the baby wanted to walk, she would hold Lucky in front of her with both hands; clearly she thought it was the stuffed rabbit that enabled her to walk.

Jane hears a high-pitched barking noise and at first she thinks it is Cato or Artemis or one of the other neighborhood dogs, but she realizes immediately that what she hears is herself, sobbing aloud. When she enters the hall, she hears another voice. It is Huggins, talking to her answering machine. " — and I can't find the envelope," he is saying in a monotone, "and there's no paper left in the Xerox and I can't, harrumph, get the tray out."

He is literally whining, and a shudder rolls over Jane's body. She feels a brief burst of pathos, knowing that Huggins feels helpless when she is not there, but the pity is momentary. "I didn't remember you saying anything about a doctor's appointment," he continues. "I don't know how much we have in the money market account and I wanted to — hruh — write a check. I thought you said — "

She yanks the telephone cord from the wall. It will be awhile before Huggins even notices the line has gone dead. He will be sitting at his desk droning on and on. Mommy, I need a drink of water, Mommy, I have to go potty.

She is light-headed, her forehead feels like a helium balloon, but her legs are like ballast and she virtually shuffles into the bedroom, her shoes rasping against the rug. She is under the bed before she knows it; the carpet under the bed is as warm and smooth as velvet and smells musty and comfortable like her grandmother's old Chesterfield sofa did when Jane visited her in Iowa as a girl. She rubs her cheek against the nap of the carpet, almost as if it were really the warm hair of Lars's chest, nuzzling. She remembers the first time he took her to bed, god, it was yesterday. "You're my baby, my beautiful baby," he whispered to her. "Baby, sweet little baby."

The smoke alarm begins beeping again in the hallway, shrieking into the silence of the room. It is punishing her for not replacing the battery last night and is now beeping more loudly and more frequently; it is deafening. She would like to get out from under the bed, to fetch the ladder and disconnect the alarm, but her body is inert, immobile. It is as if she is in the midst of one of those odd dreams in which she tries to flee but her legs will not move. She melds with the carpet, at one with it, her eyes fixed on a mouselike clump of dust under the bureau, bewitched.

guest

Jane is performing some mental calculations as she walks: If she finds the gate within the next five minutes, will she find time to loop back around to one of the bars, chug a martini and make it back in time before his plane lands?

"Where's there a bar that's open?" she hears a man's voice ask, an echo of her own thoughts. She glances up to see an anguished-looking middle-aged man hurrying along, his face flushed. He repeats his question to an airline employee, louder this time, not ashamed to expose his need. She guesses that he, too, has a nerve-shattering reunion to deal with. As he rushes toward the main bar, Jane thinks, Hope I see you there in a few minutes, champ.

She's not sure if she remembers what Patrick looks like, exactly, but it is too late now to regret inviting him to visit her. They met last year at Club Med and spent only five hours together before Jane's plane left; they have not even kissed. She remembers heavily lashed brown eyes, a mesmerizing voice, and nice legs in tennis shorts, but that's about it.

The clock runs down; she barely finds the gate in time to greet her houseguest, fear centered in her abdomen like a hairball. She cannot find him at first — a number of men stride in her direction, but none of them wears shorts or speaks to her, so she cannot pick him out by the legs or the voice. She sees a man smiling widely in her direction and realizes he has identified her. She walks up to him, hears her heels clicking, clicking on the floor. "Patrick, hello," she says. Should she shake his hand, just smile, or offer a chaste hug? Give him one of those European-style hugs, her friend had advised her: elbows out, touching lightly, head turned to one side. She tries this but he balks and she bumps awkwardly into the garment bag slung over one of his shoulders.

"Want a mint?" he asks, and she hears the nervousness in his voice. "They just handed me these mints as we were getting off."

What an imbecile, she thinks, offering a woman a *mint* for god's sake. What have I got myself into? He's handsome enough, but is that all there is to recommend him?

She declines the mint and they walk along side by side, talking about the airline and the weather and she has the urge to bolt and run. She sees the man who needed a drink jogging toward one of the incoming flight areas. His face is even redder than before and his hair looks disheveled; his expression reveals that if he has found a drink, it has done nothing for him.

"Jarlsberg — that's my favorite," Patrick says.

"Mine, too," she says, though the cheese smells foul to her now and she can barely take a bite to be polite. She says, "I'm glad you didn't think it was Swiss — most people just assume it's Swiss," but she does not care about cheese and her heart is pounding, swelling like a goiter in her chest. She tries to remember that line from Tennessee Williams — something about a heart as big as a baby's head. Her heart feels large and swollen, like the Sacred Heart of Jesus pulsing in her bosom, shimmering like a carnival crucifix that glows in the dark.

She is on autopilot, the charming hostess, the date, the It-Girl; she's going through her paces, utterly disconnected from the throbbing inside her breast. As long as I feel nothing below the navel, she thinks, I'm fine. She has put his bag on the bed in the spare room, delicately she hopes, and hung his jacket in the closet there, hoping she has made it clear he should not expect to sleep with her.

They eat cheese, admire the view — the B-of-A building and the corporate Pyramid and palm trees. He follows her out into the kitchen when she goes for a second bottle of wine, and before she knows it he's drawing her to him for a kiss. *I hunger for your porpoise mouth* — an old song from the ancient past, from the Avalon or the Fillmore — she hears it now in her head, along with the rushing of blood.

"What's wrong?" he asks, as she jerks involuntarily away from him, her lips sliding briefly against his warm neck as she does not kiss him. His voice sounds wounded, he looks closely at her as she steps backward.

"I'm sorry," she says, not able to look back at him, aware of the heat of his hands as they circle her waist.

"What is it?" His voice is soft, not insistent.

"It's been a long time," she says, looking at him now.

"How long?" he asks, pulling her to him again.

She tells him, "Years," and it is his turn to step backward this time — for an instant she feels like a sideshow freak: Reptile Woman, Fish Girl.

He knows about Lars, she told him when they met. Has he imagined that she has had a string of affairs since Lars took up residency at the cemetery?

He reads her mind, whispers, "You have to let go," his breath scalding her ear, but she shakes her head.

"You don't eat much," he says, maybe an excuse to tighten his hold on her waist. "You barely touched the cheese — you're tiny as a minute."

"I eat whole chickens," she says. "The entire thing in one sitting, without a knife or fork — I'm a savage."

"Your hands are shaking, you're probably starving," he tells her.

The burning is spreading, her belly is ablaze, it is as if she has poison oak inside. She hears a child's voice come from her throat, distant and tinny. "I'm afraid," the voice says, a little girl's voice, but what she hears the voice say is, Mommy, I'm hungry, and she feels the floor pull away from her like waves at the shore.

One night in bed, she and Lars had discovered they both loved a line from the film *Midnight Cowboy*: the repeated phrase, You're the *only* one — Joe, you're the only one. They used to whisper it to each other when they were making love, You're the *only* one. Sometimes, he would breathe the foreshortened, *Only* into her ear at just the perfect moment, and she could have sworn it was true. Other times, if they were in a public place and she did not want to be mushy in front of others, she would say to Lars, "Joe . . . " and he would wink at her, knowing the rest.

The Holy Sepulchre is the blasphemous name she has given Lars's grave at Eternal Peace. She no longer goes there every weekend — even she would consider this psychotic after five years. She goes there now on anniversaries only: the night they met, the night they pledged their troth, his birthday, the night they got back together, the night he died. She goes there at night, creeping amongst the graves from her car to his plot like some freaky ghoul, carrying a flashlight — she still gets lost every time in the dark and her hands tremble as she picks her way down the rows of graves. She shines the light on his headstone, each time hoping someone else's name will be there — that "Lars Hansen, 1951–1991, God's Sweet Angel," will no longer appear. Lars's mother is responsible for the misnomer. Jane always makes a mental edit: Lars Hansen, Satan's Sweet Disciple, the Devil's Child, Hell on Wheels, Death in Bed.

She reclines on his grave, though the granite is cold in the night air. She knows herself well enough to realize the theatrics of it are important to her — that she appreciates the image of herself prostrate on Lars's grave, the stone cross casting its shadow across her shuddering back. In a sense, she and Lars are standing off to one side chuckling together at the sight, but that does not make Lars any less dead nor her any less bereaved — it is as if they exist in parallel universes. She rubs her face against the chilly granite, presses her hips against the cold rock, sings a song in between sobs, *Do you want to be my angel, do you want to die?*

She no longer imagines she smells Lars's skin as she lies on the slab, but the smell of grass and fertilizer and stone has come to represent his scent when she's face down at the Holy Sepulchre. She brings flowers, sexy ones: peonies, dahlias, orange or lavender roses past their prime. Lars had always preferred flowers that were open wide, half-dead, bursting with just-spent vitality. You can never let go, she chided him, urging him to throw out the dying flowers that sat in vases of rancid water around his house. He laughed each time she said that. He had let go beautifully, his head flying out of the Miata like a cabbage.

Patrick is one of the smart men, one of those who realizes that the key to a difficult seduction is getting the woman's shoes off. Once the shoes are off, the underpants are usually just a whisk away. He admires the curve of her arch, the taper of her instep, whispers, "Everything about you is *narrow*," and she shudders with bliss. He kisses her arch, then examines her shoes, says, "These are fuck-me-pumps — shoes with *straps*," and she feels something below the waist for the first time in five years.

"Kiss me," he whispers, but she sucks his neck instead, biting until he cries out; her nose begins to run from the thrill of tasting his salty-sweet blood on her tongue. "Jesus Christ, you're murder," she hears him say, but he sounds as if he is a thousand feet up in the sky.

She snaps out of it, murmurs, "What about you? Is everything about *you* narrow?" and he tells her no. "So, you don't have the Irish curse?" she asks.

He doesn't miss a beat. "No I don't," he says, knowing better than to cross the line by daring her to check. His tongue slides into her mouth and for an instant she thinks she has wet her pants.

She and Lars searched for a Ramos Fizz one Sunday morning, hung over and on a lark. It has been only in the years since Lars's death that people have begun to realize that raw eggs can lead to salmonella; at that time a Ramos was a Sunday routine. None of the trendy restaurants in the neighborhood had opened for brunch that early, and most of the neighborhood bars did not open until after lunch, so they almost gave up on the idea of finding some Hair of the Dog. Then they saw it: The Four Leaf Clover Bar.

Slumming. Maybe God had punished them for that, for being arrogant, for feeling lofty. Perched there amongst the bums and down-on-their-luck alkies and sadsack working stiffs and retired merchant seamen, they had sipped their fizzes and played rock and roll on the juke box. They joked with the bartender, called him by name, aware of their Gold Cards and their advanced degrees, even as they pretended to fit in.

"It's odd that we should have discovered this place," Lars said to the bartender. "The Four Leaf Clover. Because — you know — we happen to be lucky — very very lucky."

The bartender, canny as hell, answered at once, "If you was lucky, you wouldn't be here."

A toothless woman came up to them as they laughed. "Ro-suhs? Ro-suhs?" she asked, holding out a plastic bucket full of water and single roses in varying degrees of decrepitude. Lars picked the bloom most moribund, full blown and voluptuous, pink as a tongue.

"A briar rose," he said, passing the blossom beneath Jane's nose before placing it in front of her. The gin had gone to her head, Lars's hand to her thigh, and she couldn't help it, she thought: It's no accident we're in this Lucky Bar — I'm the luckiest woman alive, a dream girl, passed away and gone to heaven. I want to stay here in the Four Leaf Clover with Lars, forever.

Last night she surprised Patrick by making him sleep in the guest room, after all; Jane had put the brakes on after her shoes came off. Now she and Patrick have left the breakfast dishes on the kitchen table and are making out on her bed. She can see that Patrick imagines she banned him from her bedroom the night before simply as a strategic move, convoluted foreplay, and that now he is moving in for the kill. His mouth on hers is as hot as her groin and she is floating as if in some sort of dope dream, but then she's back in high school — she feels his hand on the hooks to her bra. "No way," she mumbles into his mouth, and he removes his lips from hers and his hand from her bra.

"Why not?" — he looks baffled.

"The abyss," she answers, and he stares at her as if she is crazed. She is not ready to fall into that black hole, to give herself over. "A person can be a virgin twice," she says. Before he can answer her, she puts her tongue deep into his mouth, sucking, thrusting her hips against his pelvis, falling, but not all the way into the pit.

"God! The things you do," he says, "for someone who . . ."

Yes, she knows, she's a hot slut, for someone who won't take off her underwear.

She imagines herself eating and eating: not just an entire deli chicken, but weighty blocks of cheese, pounds of Jarlsberg and brie, massive sandwiches on sour dough rolls, salami squishing under her teeth, grazing her palate with its peppery, garlicky bite, the hard rolls fracturing and sending crumbs in all directions, the lettuce cool and fresh, the mustard tangy with Maui onions, the tomatoes slithering against her tongue. She envisions herself lying in bed weighing eight hundred pounds like the man in New York who needed a crane to haul him to the hospital. She wants this, wants to revel in sensation, wallow in flesh.

She used to see a young man on the Muni bus; she always thought of him as the Lover. He was with a different woman every time she saw him, but each time he acted as if the girl were the only one. The girls were all beautiful, though not as exotic as the Lover himself. The Lover's skin was deep olive, his eyes heavy lidded and greedy, his lips curved up and out in a way she thought of as European; he wore his long shiny black hair in a ponytail, an earring in one ear — not Jane's usual type at all. He had his arm around the girl each time, his face no more than two inches from hers. Yes, he was handsome as a god, but that wasn't all — it was the way he managed to tune out the entire world for the girl and him — he created an island of passion for the two of them on the bus. You're the only one, he would whisper to her, would kiss her behind the ear, would tilt her chin up with one hand and look into her face for the longest time, would kiss her softly on the lips, pull her close. He spent the entire bus ride looking into the woman's eyes as if bewitched — the girl always had to watch for their stop or they would have ridden all the way to the end of the line.

Jane had wanted the Lover, but at the same time she was revolted by him. She wondered if Lars murmured into the ears of other women, made each one feel as if she were Helen of Troy. Once, Lars rode the bus for a few blocks with her when they went over to North Beach for coffee, and she saw the Lover and his latest woman sitting a few seats ahead of them.

"Look at that guy," she said to Lars. "I think he's terribly handsome and intriguing — he's with a different girl every time — look at them necking." She had expected Lars to laugh, to say that the guy looked gay, but he had not.

"Yes," Lars had said, immediately, "He's cool; he looks like a young Yves Montand." She never saw the Lover again after that, and soon she stopped watching for him.

Patrick does not really know her, she thinks — they had spent only that one afternoon together when they met last summer and have kept their phone calls and letters on the level of light flirtation. He does not understand as Lars did that she will bite, suck, spank, demand, lick, trash-talk, beg, and yet in the next instant will be too modest to dress in front of him, will blush at the word ass. You convent girls are always the biggest tramps, she remembers a boy in her hometown saying to her.

When Patrick offers a condom the first time, she hisses, "Don't taint things."

"That's crazy!"

"I need to feel you," she tells him, throwing the condom across the room and pulling him to her. They make love all over the house — it is almost as if Lars is back. They break and stain the furniture, knock over dishes and glasses, leave the stereo turned high so the neighbors cannot hear their cries.

Afterward he says, "You're bleeding, Janie," alarmed.

She answers, "You didn't believe me."

"Are you sure it's not that time of the month?" he insists, but she shakes her head and they both fall silent.

Later he says, "You're killing me — they'll have to take me to the airport in an ambulance," and she thinks, if anyone has taken Lars's place, it's me.

But Patrick is killing her, too, it seems — she has the shakes and a terrible, grinding abdominal pain. She sneaks into the bedroom when he is in the shower and telephones a woman friend of hers, a physician. "Help me," she whispers, "I'm in trouble." She blurts the entire litany: "I have a horrible stomach ache — I'm doubled-over. I can't stop shaking — I'm a wreck. Help me — I need meds — god, you have to help me!" Patrick drives to the pharmacy for her while she lies curled up sideways on the sofa, rocking.

Years ago, after a long weekend with Lars, she went to the dictionary and looked up satyr. No, Lars was not half-man, half-goat, nor was he a "licentious man, a lecher." The word satyriasis was just beneath it: excessive, often uncontrollable sexual desire in a man. That was closer to the mark, she thought, but what did that make her? There was no comparable word, unless it was nympho, which certainly could not apply to a woman who had slept with less than a handful of men in her life.

"You're the only woman who's ever been able to go the distance," Lars had told her.

Jane had a momentary vision of herself in running attire with a number on her chest, then asked, "What do you mean?"

"None of them could keep going," he told her "— not like you. They'd get too tired, too sore, too overstimulated, too offended, too something. You're the only one — the only one who always keeps going."

The truth was, it had terrified Jane to look at the clock and realize that she and Lars had been in bed, awake, for eighteen hours — that the sheets were drenched in a clichéd mixture of blood, sweat, tears, and wine — that they were trembling and smoking cigarettes and lying in the pool of warm cream sherry that Lars had poured on her body.

Maybe her gluttony could have been predicted. She remembered the incident with the See's candy, certainly a clue. Someone had left a box of chocolates on her desk at the office, a thank-you gift for something, and she sat there with the office door closed and consumed the entire two pounds. When she went outside a few minutes later for an errand, she felt herself flushing, her chest and face turning red and a steamy burning rising up from beneath her clothing. Maybe I'm allergic, she thought, overcome by dizziness. She leaned against an office building, the marble facade cool against her heated face.

"Are you all right, miss?" a passerby asked.

She told him, "Yes, I just felt faint for a moment." My god, I'm out of control, she thought, her pulse the speed of light.

This is Patrick's last night as her house guest; he flies out in the morning. A romantic dinner would have been nice, but she cannot miss the Tyson fight. She decides on an Irish sports bar with closed circuit, thinking this will be colorful for an out-of-towner. The sedatives have kicked in and her stomach has stopped roiling, but she feels as if she is cushioned in Styrofoam. She takes Patrick into the supermarket with her a few hours before the fight, asking him to choose some wine while she picks up a few items. He comes up behind her when she is buying paper towels, presses his body against hers, says, "Come over here — I want to show you something." He takes her by the hand and pulls her to the delicatessen section. He points at the line of barbecued chickens gleaming in a row beneath a plastic sneeze guard.

"Are those the chickens you eat whole?" he asks. He bends forward to pick up a chicken, says, "I have to see you scarf one of these—I've yet to see you put a bite of food into your mouth."

Her heart rate accelerates as if it has been jump-started by one of those plungerlike devices she has seen on TV. "No!" she says, pulling him away from the chicken.

He laughs, clearly teasing her from the start, and says, "Jane, you're adorable.

"I'm a savage," she tells him again, "Enter at your own risk."

She walks away from the deli counter and suddenly thinks of her mother's underwear drawer: full of brand new silk and satin underwear, boxes of stashed candies, latex girdles. The smell of chocolate and silk.

Jane is intrigued at having their hands stamped after they pay to watch the closed-circuit boxing match. Patrick seems delighted by the diversity of the crowd—she has forgotten that not all cities are this eclectic. They find a spot at a long table, sandwiched amongst straight and gay couples, old codgers and college kids, everyone festive. "Jell-O shots? Jell-O shots—three dollars," she hears a woman call out like a newsboy on the street. Jane looks up and sees a red-haired waitress carrying a huge tray filled with white paper cups of green Jell-O, topped with whipped cream. She has heard about this—vodka in Jell-O—but had not quite believed it, had thought it a pagan concept: wolfing down booze, pretending you're not even drinking.

"I have to do this," she says to Patrick, and he pays the barmaid even as he asks, "Are you sure?"

She nods, though she is thinking, I'm already getting seriously fucked-up. The sedatives she has begged from her doctor friend mingle in her bloodstream with the wine she drank earlier.

The lime gelatin in the Jell-O shot reminds her again of her mother—of finding green jelly beans hidden under the sofa cushions. Her mother had kept food hidden in the oddest places. When Jane was growing up, she would find snacks sequestered all over the house:

candy buried in the bureau; cookies in the trunk of the car; packages of potato chips and corn nuts in the linen closet. Jane and her sisters were not allowed to eat a bite of food without asking permission of their mother, and they never touched a morsel between meals. Her mother ran a tight ship: no conspicuous consumption tolerated.

She glances about, watches what others are doing with the Jell-O shots, but they seem to be swallowing the entire cupful whole and then wiping the whipped cream off their lips with the backs of their hands, and she cannot see herself doing this. "Sir, can you hand me a napkin?" she asks a man sitting near a dispenser on the table, and she nibbles as daintily as possible at the trembling green blob in her cup, feeling giddy even before the vodka slides down her throat. "This is *fun*," she says.

Patrick squeezes her tight, whispers, "How am I ever going to be able to say goodbye to you?"

She smiles, says nothing, thinks, Any old way, easy as swallowing Jell-O, swallowing you.

Tyson comes onto the screens, sixteen of them, that line the walls of the bar. Every way she turns, she sees him walking toward her, huge and centered and glistening, sixteen times, sixteen ways.

"Wow, Tyson's menacing," she hears Patrick say, but she is surfing the tide of numbness now, sensation blurred, one step removed. She sees at once that Tyson is in a similar mode: His focus is deeply in place; he is above and away from the fray; his body sways softly as he walks to the ring, his carriage somewhere between a gladiator's stance and a pimp-roll. I know you, she thinks, and when he begins to pummel his opponent, a look of blood-lust in his eyes, she says Yes. She strokes Patrick's thigh, listening to all the voices in the bar shout "Good one!" and "Go-go-go!"

When Patrick does not kiss her in response to her touch nor tighten his arm around her waist, she turns and looks at him, but discovers that she has mistakenly been stroking the thigh of an old geezer sitting in a chair just behind Patrick's and her chairs. The geezer has said nothing. "Oh, I'm so sorry," she says, pulling her hand away as if burned.

Jane had taken a taxi home from the New Year's Eve party after slapping Lars's face in the host's kitchen. The next morning, she went to the supermarket and bought deli sandwiches and beer; she and Lars usually watched the football games on New Year's Day. She knew they would make up — they always did — but she realized she might have to eat some crow after slapping him. She picked up a bottle of Mumm's and decided to take it over to Lars's apartment a little later. Hello, darling, she would say — I've come to celebrate our making up: Happy New Year. If he resisted, she would whisper into his ear, You're the only one. When she returned home from the store, she discovered a message on her answering machine from Lars's brother: Jane, you'd better call me when you get this message — there's been an accident.

"I don't do goodbyes," she tells Patrick as he drives her car to the airport. She says it to have an excuse to leave him at the curb rather than seeing him off at the gate, but her words are a lie. Not saying goodbye is far worse — that much she knows. Still, the thought of breaking down in front of him mortifies Jane, so she finds herself giving Patrick a false smile that feels like a rictus and he looks somewhat alarmed. "You don't mind if I just drop you off and we skip all the maudlin stuff, do you?" she asks, and Patrick says that, no, he doesn't mind. A longish silence fills the car.

He drives up in front of the departing flights area and turns to Jane, starts to say something, but she cuts him off.

"Hop out," she says, stonewalling him, "and I'll slide right over." She begins sliding over to press her point and he obliges her by getting out; she quickly pulls the door closed. He has a strained look on his face and again begins to speak, but she says through the window glass, "Just go."

She grinds the car into gear and lurches it forward. Tears sting her eyes behind the dark glasses and she cannot quite see Patrick — she nearly runs him over. She catches a glance of shock and outrage on his face as the car bears down on him and she slams on the brakes.

"I *told* you to be careful," she calls out the window. She thinks, Oh god, I almost put you in the Holy Sepulchre, too, didn't I? She does not dare to look back or wave to him, and composes an on-the-spot mantra: It's not love — it's just lust; it's not love — it's just lust, and says it over and over again like an automaton. By the twentieth time, the tears have stopped, but she finds herself taking the freeway directly from the airport to the cathedral.

A man driving ahead of her in the lane off to her right has painted a slogan on the back of his car in day-glo paint. "BASS PLAYERS DO IT DEEP," she reads, and steps on the accelerator. She pulls up alongside him, drives parallel with him, looks him in the face, and smirks suggestively before changing lanes and speeding off.

She sits in a pew toward the back so she can sneak out early if she chooses. A lapsed Catholic who attends Episcopal services when she is troubled, she gets all the glitz of her former church, without confession and kneeling and nuns. She has never been able to pray for Lars; she knows nothing she could say to God would affect his spot in the hereafter. If she is honest with herself, she admits she is too mean spirited to pray for him, angry that he has left her.

A woman in a floor-length purple robe approaches the altar carrying a long-handled taper to light the candles before the service begins. Jane does not know exactly what the woman is called; surely she's not a priest, nor an altar boy, though she looks like the latter with her cropped hair. She lights each candle, carrying the long pole from one side of the altar to the other and then walks off to the right. Clack! Jane looks toward the noise, which turns out to be the polelike taper hitting the stone steps as the purple-robed cleric falls down.

In order to stave off the fit of laughter she feels coming on, Jane has to pretend she is praying. Good god, she cannot laugh in church at a woman falling on her butt! She squeezes her eyes shut, bows her head, reins herself in, clasps her hands tightly together. She fears that in spite of herself a sardonic smile twists at her face. She remembers how hard she laughed when she found out Lars had been decapitated, the way the image of his head leaving the car had triggered a macabre spasm of giggling.

She half-listens to the dean of the cathedral. "Free your spirit from the dungeon you have built for yourself," he says, his voice resonating off the stone walls.

She had carried the bottle of champagne she bought for Lars's and her rapprochement out to the garbage chute in the hall of her apartment building and hurled it down, listening to it bonk against the chute all the way to the bottom.

She takes communion, needing to merge. Body of Christ — she opens her mouth when she hears these words, but realizes at once she has made an error. She is standing there with her mouth open like a starving baby bird, but the protocol in this church is to cup one's hands to receive the Host. She closes her mouth, opens her hands, opens her mouth again and pops the tidbit in: She cannot help it — she knows a cracker when she tastes one; it's not the Body of Christ. And when she drinks from the chalice, she tastes only wine, even imagines she feels a slight buzz. The wine seems closer to Tokay than to the Blood of Christ — it slides down her throat, so warm — she cannot help thinking of Patrick. She cherishes the leap of faith she makes when sipping from the same chalice that everyone else drinks from, parishioners with hepatitis and HIV and who knows what else? She pretends to pray again, and soon she cannot tell the fake prayers from the genuine; her heart opens out.

The Jiffy-Mart provided everything she needs: a refill of the prescription for sedatives, a strong laxative, boxes of lime Jell-O, Redi-Whip, Stoli, and rotisserie chicken.

She pours boiling water over the powder, watching it turn green as she stirs the mixture in the glass bowl. She uses only half the amount of water the directions call for, substitutes Stoli for the rest—she hopes this is the way to do this Jell-O–shot thing.

Before the feast she goes into the spare room, pulls back the blankets and lies down where Patrick slept the first night, before they were lovers. She inhales his scent, familiar to her now, soon to be forgotten, and presses her cheek against a few strands of hair she finds on the sheets. She kisses the spot where he lay, a private thing, no one need know.

The vodka makes a pleasant glugging noise as she pours it into a tumbler, and the chicken releases a fragrant steam into the kitchen when she removes the plastic wrapper. She tears off a drumstick, yanking it hard, takes a long hard pull at the tumbler of vodka. Yes.

Formal like a guest; Falling apart like thawing ice; It is because she is not full that she can be worn and yet newly made.

magdalena

blood bank

Magda takes a bus to the blood bank on her lunch break. It's only about ten blocks from her office, not worth taking a cab, but she's too tired to walk that far. She sees a teenager on the bus with a pacifier hanging from his neck on a string. She is mesmerized, wondering what this means. He is wearing headphones and listening to music she cannot hear, a dreamy look on his face. She looks over at his friend, another teenaged boy, wearing those below-the-knee shorts that she's been noticing on kids lately. The friend has a baby bottle hanging from a short chain attached to his belt. She remembers then that she has seen this trend mentioned in a style magazine she thumbed through at the facial salon. Pacifiers and baby bottles have become icons of the teens; they wear them the way Magda wore a peace symbol when she was young.

The boy with the bottle sees her looking at him and gives her what she perceives as a haughty smirk, so she looks rapidly away. She tries to decide what it is that these bottles and pacifiers are supposed to indicate, exactly. Some sort of sucking metaphor, surely. Could it have something to do with homosexuality, or just sex in general? She decides it is probably more than that, that the kids just wish to regress, go back to infancy. The poor things don't even have their own music, she thinks. They listen to Led Zeppelin and Pink Floyd, old business, stuff their parents listened to when they were young.

She is on the way to donate blood for herself, for her forthcoming surgery. It's the way people do things these days, having their own blood taken and then put back into them after surgery. Her best friend donated a pint for Magda, but received a postcard back from the blood bank telling her she was positive for Hepatitis C and that the blood could not be used. It had offended her friend to be told she was tainted in some way, and Magda had felt an ugly strain on their friendship. Magda's mother had told her many times when she was growing up, "If you want something done right, Magda, you have to do it yourself."

She has chosen a downtown branch of the blood bank, not wishing to go all the way across town and donate at the large, institutional-type center with bleak rows of cots. The financial district blood bank is in one of the older high-rise buildings, and when she gets out of the elevator she thinks at first that she has come to the wrong place. She walks by accountants' offices and land developers' offices and finally finds a room with the number the lady gave her over the telephone. There is a small brass plate on the door stating that this is a blood bank branch, but she has to take off her dark glasses in order to read it. She wears bifocals now, the "progressive" kind without the line in the middle, but sometimes she has trouble reading small print anyway.

They give her papers to fill out, and then she sits in a chair reading *Newsweek* while she waits. It is more like a dentist's waiting room than it is a bank, or maybe even like a unisex hair salon, where men and women sit nervously together in chairs reading magazines while they wait for their turn. But the room is nothing at all like a bank, and she laughs at herself now for expecting that it would be. How long had she carried around in her mind the image of a large, drafty marble lobby, with jars of bright red blood stored in vaults, or lined up on shelves like tomatoes preserved in Mason jars?

Finally a pretty, older black woman calls her name, "Magdalena Portman?" in a contralto voice. She hears her own voice come out tight and high, pinched, "Yes," as she gets to her feet.

"Right this way," the woman says, and indicates another chair in a small cubicle where Magda is to sit down. She explains that before subjecting her to withdrawal of an entire pint, she will first draw a little of Magda's blood for screening. While she is swabbing Magda's arm and getting the paraphernalia ready, the woman looks over Magda's information card and reads off the names of the drugs she has listed there as "medications routinely or occasionally taken."

"Xanax," the woman says rather loudly, "My sister's been taking that, but she says it doesn't really help."

"Some things can't be helped by taking a pill," Magda replies, blushing. She wonders what might have happened to the woman's sister to precipitate taking tranquilizers, anti-anxiety agents as they are more commonly known.

The woman looks at her. "Oh oh," she says, "Your hematocrit looks a little low, dear."

Magda is stunned. "What do you mean?"

"You're a little iron-poor," she explains. "We're going to have to test this another time before we can accept blood from you. I'm gonna take this sample in back and spin it—I want you to wait in the canteen." She gestures toward a group of tables and chairs in the back of the room.

She does not know what the woman means about spinning, and imagines her blood whirling crazily in the back room like some mystical fluid dervish.

She now realizes why her friend was insulted when her blood was rejected. She too feels embarrassed and deficient to be sent off to the "canteen," an oddly militaristic term for the table full of donuts and orange juice and crackers and cheese. Iron-poor in the blood bank, it seems to her that the more robust donors stare curiously at her as she walks back to the canteen.

"Have some cheese and crackers with your juice," the woman calls out to her, and Magda mumbles that she's not hungry, thinking that if she were going to submit to several hundred unwanted calories, it wasn't going to be for some funky crackers and processed cheese in a blood bank canteen. "I think you'd better eat something," the woman insists, "Some *cheese.*"

Magda's face flames, and she thinks, Well, there's plenty of blood left in my body after all. She opens the packet of crackers and cheese, docile, actually eating the tasteless yellow "cheddar," chewing, bovine and passive. There is a cactus plant in a colorful ceramic pot near the screen that separates the canteen from the blood-drawing area, and as Magda looks at it, she remembers the time she and Brent took the ferry to La Paz for Christmas, the first year they were married. They had driven on to Cabo San Lucas for some fishing — Brent's stock-broker owned a beach house there and they had the whole place to themselves for a week. It had been a relaxing time for them, drinking margaritas on the ferry, singing Feliz Navidad along with the band in the bar on the boat; swimming and fishing and letting the Mexican caretaker at the beach house serve them ceviche made from fresh lime juice and fish they caught themselves.

When they were driving back to the border, Brent had suddenly stopped the car and gone to the trunk for a shovel. He started digging up a tall cactus plant as casually as if he were working in their garden back in Sausalito. "What are you doing?" she called from the car, and he looked up with a sly, venal smile.

"Do you know how much a cactus this size sells for at home?" he said. "This is perfect for that sunny corner in the dining room. It's green gold — I'm bagging it."

"They said we couldn't take any plants or seeds over the border," she reminded him.

"You tend to be kind of a hard-liner sometimes, Maggie, you know that? Rules can be bent."

"But they belong to Mexico," she said. "It's sort of like stealing, isn't it?"

Brent sighed. "If you want to get technical, they belong to God," he said. "They're ours as much as anybody else's."

Brent looked like a grave digger to her as he shoveled sand. When he finished digging up the plant, she stood depressed and quiet by the side of the Volvo while he wrapped it gently in a blanket and hid it under the back seat. Brent the philosopher, concealing God's cactus. He swore to the border guards with an earnest look that there was nothing in the car, nothing to declare. She has always wondered how the guards knew he was lying, but they were asked to get out of the car while the guards methodically searched the trunk, then looked under the seats with flashlights. When they found the plant, Brent said he must have "forgotten" about it. Maybe the guards had expected to find drugs and the cactus was an anticlimax, because after confiscating the plant they just shook their heads disgustedly and let them go. Brent had been annoyed and aloof, but Magda felt like a thief in a pillory on the village green.

"Magdalena Portman?" calls a sonorous voice. It is the nice woman who drew her blood, gesturing to Magda to come back to the cubicle and sit down. She notices for the first time that the woman wears a name tag, "Carmen," on her pink smock.

"No wonder you have such a nice voice," she says, pointing to the name tag. She feels foolish for getting personal, but the woman smiles.

"My mother was a real opera fan," she says. "You know what, though, we're not going to be able to take your blood today." She thumbs through the paperwork and says, "If you took some iron and came back another time, maybe, but I see your surgery is only a week from now — it doesn't look as if we'll be able to get your count up high enough by then. Can you get another donor, hon?"

"Do you mean that I'm too weak to give blood to *myself*?" Magda asks. "I mean, I guess if I'm a little anemic, maybe no one else would want my blood, but if it's for me, what's the difference?" She feels panicked, on the verge of sobbing. She sees from the expression on Carmen's face that she is coming off as uncooperative, truculent.

"You need all the blood you have, girl. And maybe more. It's for your own protection," she says. "Get yourself some iron tablets to build yourself up for the surgery, and ask somebody else to donate for you, OK?"

As Magda picks up her handbag and rises to leave, the woman says, "Good luck with your surgery, dear," and Magda does cry then, touched by the sincerity in the woman's voice.

I am going to be gutted like a fish, she thinks as she walks back to the bus stop. But there is a moment of hilarity for her out of nowhere: She sees a car parked illegally in the bus zone, and on the back bumper is a large sticker —

BUSINESS IS GREAT
PEOPLE ARE FANTASTIC!
GOD IS WONDERFUL

Oh my goodness, she thinks, the poor fool.

The Cheshire Cat appears when she is in the midst of a dope-dream. Probably the doctors would call it something else: morphine-induced dissociative reaction, or something like that, but it is a dope-dream nonetheless. His smile is so large, so floaty, that it is impossible not to think of the Cheshire Cat, even though she had always hated *Alice in Wonderland* and been frightened by the story as a child.

"Hello," he says, beaming familiarly, and she is certain that she is supposed to know who he is.

"Hi," she says, smiling falsely, biding her time. She presses down on the little button that looks like a "Jeopardy!" buzzer and sends another burst of morphine into her bloodstream. The pain is still formidable under the narcotic haze.

"How ya doin, dear?" the Cheshire Cat asks, smiling messianically.

"Great, nice of you to stop by," she says, wondering who the hell he is and why she cannot place him. She is surprised that she would have a visitor with such a salesmanlike smile and snake-oil veneer to him. She feels herself start to nod out, then forces herself to keep smiling back at him. Her eyelids do drop closed for a moment, but she jerks herself awake again. She makes a tremendous effort to go along with the charade, hoping she'll remember any moment just who he might be.

"I'm Pastor Chatham," he says, "Pastor Chet Chatham — what's your name, honey?"

"Magda," she hears herself say, the voice faraway and tinny.

"I'm a people-person, Magda," he says. "I like to meet people. I'm here visiting Trudy and I thought I'd just come over and make your acquaintance. What kind of surgery did you have?"

"No way," she hears the metallic voice say. She is not sure what she means, but Pastor Chatham catches her gist immediately.

"Too personal sweetheart? That's OK, I understand. You just keep it to yourself, now, if that's what makes you more comfortable. Are you a Christian, Magda?" She remembers now that her roommate on the other side of the curtain in the adjacent bed belongs to a fundamentalist sect, that she told her about being "saved" when they talked through the curtain in the middle of the night after their surgeries.

Am I a Christian? She doesn't think about it, just floats above the question and listens to herself answer in a friendly tone, almost with a western drawl, "More or less, I guess." She imagines that she has actually said, "I 'spect so," and bitten off a chaw of tobacco.

The reverend takes it in stride, however, and asks, "Do you pray?"

"No."

"Would you mind if I prayed for you? Would you pray with me and my wife and Trudy?"

She does not wish to offend her roommate Trudy by being rude to her pastor. "I won't pray with you, but it would be fine if you want to pray," she says, leaving out the words "for me."

He turns his head toward the other side of the room, the portion behind the curtain, his smile becoming a wedge in profile. "Magda here isn't a rabid atheist, so she's gonna let us pray for her," he says. Mrs. Chet Chatham steps forward. "Let us pray," the reverend says, his voice powerful and full of the fact that he is accustomed to calling the shots. Magda bows her head instantly, closes her eyes, not so much out of piety as much as a way of not having to look at the Chathams during the prayer.

"Dear God," he prays, "We are here with Trudy and Magda in the hospital, and we ask that in your infinite and tender mercy, you will help them recover from their surgery. We ask, Heavenly Father, that you heal our sisters Trudy and Magda, ease their pain, and that you help them grow strong again, help them become whole. Amen."

"Thank you, Pastor," she whispers, feeling a bit mawkish. When tears come to her eyes, she is furious with this redneck for putting her in such a position. She pushes the morphine button again, but it's too soon and nothing comes out. She goes with her visceral urge. "God is wonderful," she says to the pastor, and as he advances toward her with his auto-row smile glimmering, she continues, "People are fantastic! Business is great."

Pastor Chet Chatham is not a stupid man, for he flinches and looks closely at her. "God bless you," he says curtly and takes Mrs. Chatham by the arm and they leave.

You were a few hours late, Rev, she thinks. Even prayer can't make me whole.

Her sister Holly has driven her home from the hospital and is bustling about the kitchen. Just as Holly was matron of honor at Magda's wedding, and drove her to the emergency room when she started having a miscarriage while Brent was away on business, she has also come through for her now. She came up with the blood for the transfusion, and now she is making tea, setting tiny cookies out on a plate, and putting tube roses into a vase all at the same time. "Can you think of anything else I should get from the pharmacy or the grocery before I have to go pick the kids up from school?" Holly asks, but Magda tells her she stocked the house thoroughly before the surgery. She watches Holly cheerfully performing chores for her and feels guilty for being morose and mopey. She knows it is simply a form of perverse vanity that is making her feel so sorry for herself: She had never in her wildest dream thought she would become the kind of woman who has to take a taxi to the hospital, who is looked after by sisters and aunts, whose body is no longer the object of young mens' lust, but who instead has been reamed out, hacked up, defeminized. "At least I still have my breasts," she says to Holly.

"Amen," Holly says.

"Please!" Magda shrieks. "You sound like Pastor Chet Chatham, the praying Cheshire Cat."

"What you see depends on where you are, doesn't it?" Holly asks, turning to her with a teacup balanced on a saucer and a dreamy look on her face. "A lunar eclipse would be a solar eclipse if you were on the moon."

They laugh and drink tea and talk about everything in the world except the fact that subsequent to a brief trip to the pathology lab, her womb has been discarded in the trash bins out behind the hospital, just the way the ugly clumps of red gloppy stuff, "tissue" they called it, had been tossed into the same bins after each miscarriage. Little Brent and two Little Magdas, splat, over and out, fini, off to the landfill.

There is no way she can avoid her father's telephone calls now. He knows she has to lie in bed for three full weeks, so Whitey will not be fooled if she leaves the answering machine on and does not answer the telephone. He has become a pest in his dotage, transformed from a tough guy and a bully into a whining child. Her mother is completely deaf now, so Whitey telephones Magda nearly daily just to have someone who can hear him complain.

"How are you feeling, Magda?" he asks, then begins talking about his knee replacement surgery before she can answer. It doesn't matter: She knows the only answer acceptable to Whitey would have been, "Fine." Her father has no patience with anyone who is in pain, and even in the midst of his own lengthy litanies of grievances, he will interject, "I'm fine!" or "I'm not *sick*, mind you."

"I saw in the paper that Brent got a big promotion," Whitey says.

She had seen it too in the financial section that morning. "BRENT PORTMAN NAMED MANAGING PARTNER OF TRANS-CYBER," the caption said, with a picture of Brent smiling, showing his newly bleached and bonded teeth. He's begun to go bald, but he has enough money now so that he does not need hair in order to attract women. She hears on the grapevine that he still plays around behind the back of his second wife.

"They gave him a big car, ya know," Whitey tells her, "And they're sending him to the big head office — he has all the big accounts."

Big is Whitey's word, now that he has begun to shrivel up. He loves big in his second childhood. He boasts of the big muscles in his withered arms and legs, tells her what big men his doctors and accountants are. Even her mother's physical therapist is a big, tall woman whose husband is a big shot on the county board of supervisors.

"Yes, Brent is doing well," she says blandly.

Whitey says, "I guess he'll spend it all on those big galoot sons he has with that Oriental gal."

How did it go? she tries to remember. Was it "sans hair, sans teeth, sans everything"?

Whitey is complaining now, going on and on about his digestive problems and about "her" — meaning her mother — and about how none of the kids visits them anymore, etc., and she wishes she felt sorry for him, but she cannot. Whitey is an emotional hooligan who has no one left to torment except her mother, who no longer hears a word he says; he is retired by default from his career as a brute. She wants to think of him as "the poor old thing," but images float up in front of her face when she sees or hears her father, float up like the messages that bobbed to the surface of her Magic Eight-Ball when she was a girl.

The image that floats up now is that of tentacles. She had been nine years old and still pining over the puppy her parents had gotten rid of one day when she was in school. She had been begging for another puppy, a smaller, more suitable one that they could keep, so when her father greeted her one afternoon when she came home and said, "I have something to show you," she thought she had prevailed. There was an air of excitement about him, and his face was red beneath his white shock of hair.

"Is it . . . ?" she'd asked him breathlessly, afraid to say the word dog, but he'd ignored her. She knew something out of the ordinary was going on, because normally Whitey would be at work in the afternoon, so she figured there was a special event in the offing — maybe her mother and father had gone to the puppy farm while she was in school.

"In the garage," he said. "A surprise." Whitey's face was mysterious and she trailed after him to the garage, knowing it had to be a dog — it couldn't be anything else. Her father was wearing denims and a sweater and rubber-soled shoes instead of his usual wing tips. Her mother joined them, loping along beside them to the garage. "You're not going to believe this," she told Magda.

She saw nothing when she entered the garage, blinking as they left the sunny driveway and went into the darkened space, then looking blindly ahead of her when her father switched on the ceiling bulb. She saw nothing at first, then recoiled as she heard a thud. She did not see anything except her father's blue Chevy, but she heard guffawing from the loft overhead.

"Can't you see it?" Whitey asked. "Or don't you believe your eyes?"

"On the top of Dad's car," her mother prompted.

She stared at the Chevrolet. The roof of the car seemed almost to move and teem, but she could not really focus on anything, was so seized by the idea of a dog that she could see nothing but the absence of a puppy.

From the loft overhead came a voice, "It's an octopus!" and another guffaw. She looked up to see their neighbor Biff Sanchez smiling and laughing; she realized at once that he had thrown something from the loft when she heard the thud.

The rest was a blur — she never really did get a good look at the unfortunate creature before she fled the garage. She learned later that the Octopus Vulgaris, the most intelligent of all invertebrate animals, can change its color and texture like a chameleon, so perfectly that it becomes almost identical to its background. Whitey and Biff Sanchez had gone sport fishing on the bay that day and somehow had come home with an octopus in a canvas bag in the trunk of Biff's car. Throwing it from the loft onto the roof of Whitey's Chevy to frighten Magda was their idea of great fun, a wonderful practical joke. She knew they left the beast in the garage to die, to perish in the dank air, out of its element, its gills trembling in shock. Whitey ended up getting extra mileage out of the joke by putting the corpse on top of the garbage can, its eight tentacled arms draped over the receptacle to scare the scavengers in the morning.

"You sure don't take after your father," Whitey is saying now on the other end of the telephone. Before she can indulge herself in an outburst of laughter, he goes on to tell her, "You wouldn't catch me laying flat on my back after surgery — I'm no quitter."

Her first response is nearly primordial, it dates so far back — she has an impulse to defend herself, to blurt out, "I *haven't* quit!" but she stifles every impulse except the one to stonewall her father. "Yeah," he says. "They can't keep a good man down. When I had the bilateral knee replacement, I was out walking in the hall without crutches two days later — the hospital is going to do a study on my recuperative powers."

She realizes then for the first time that the tablets they sent home with her from the hospital are stronger than she'd thought. She feels almost as if she is about to be unconscious. She closes her eyes and there is Whitey's face in the reddish-black space that becomes her field of vision. There is a rope around Whitey's neck, pulling tighter and tighter, squeezing the breath from him. But, no, it is not really a rope, but a tentacled thing, the phantom arm of an Octopus Vulgaris, choking the life out of her father, the little suction cups on the tentacles grabbing at the skin on her father's neck, sucking like some vampire infant suckling.

She hangs up the receiver on the telephone without replying to her father, though she hears him nattering away. She unplugs the telephone so that if he calls back it will just ring on and on. She slides down onto her pillow, drifting like a prom queen waltzing, but before she falls asleep she pulls up her nightgown and peers beneath the steri-strip over her incision. The bloody groove beneath the wide plastic band is like an ugly gaping mouth above her mound of Venus, but she laughs breathily before she drifts into sleep, because if she looks at the scar with her eyes squinted, it looks like nothing in the world except an upside-down smile, a leering smiley-face sticker, "Have A Nice Day!"

Magda is now ambulatory, after three weeks in bed which passed rather quickly, neither a trial nor a relief, but just a respite, a way station. There was a time when weeks and weeks without sex would have been unthinkable, unbearable, but the fact was that in the years since the divorce, this has become the norm. "A woman of a certain age" is an expression one hears. In France, it means a woman who is spicy, cooking in her own juices as she enters mid-life. In the United States, the definition of the phrase is "over the hill."

She stands at the bar at Tosca, waiting for Holly, drinking a brandied cappuccino. It has been four weeks since the surgery, the "procedure," her doctor called it, and she has managed to work a few mornings at the office. Fatigued and pale, she gets uncomfortable when she sits too long. She and Holly have planned to lunch in the neighborhood and then Holly will drive her home. A glance at her Swatch tells her that Holly is late, but Magda knows parking is difficult in North Beach.

The man on the stool next to where she is standing sees her look at the watch and asks chummily, "Someone let you down?"

"Not *today*," she responds, and they both laugh. He is so obviously from out of town that she does not have the heart to be curt with him. She had been amused when she first came in to notice that the poor bastard had found "I Left My Heart in San Francisco" on the jukebox stocked with primarily operatic selections and actually chosen to play it.

"Do you enjoy Tony?" he asks her with an accent that she takes to be New Jersey.

"Tony?" She thinks of that interesting man in Great Britain, but he was divorced out of the royal family long ago, she knows.

"Bennett," he says, still dazzled by the "little cable cars."

"I never thought about it," she says, but then tells him the truth.

"He pronounces San Francisco incorrectly. We don't say *fran*cisco, we say frunSISco."

"You a native?" he asks, and for a moment she relishes the image of herself naked with a spear in the jungle before she nods and says that, yes, she was born here.

"Family?"

Does he think I care to make small talk with a hairy stranger from Hoboken, does he think it's come to that? She feels herself begin to ride the same wave that had carried her along with Pastor Chet Chatham in the hospital. "I have a sister," she says, "I'm waiting for her now — she'll be here in a couple of minutes." The man orders another cappuccino and asks her if she would like one too but she shakes her head no. "My parents are dead," she says. He doesn't seem to be paying that much attention, is nodding politely while he shoves currency toward the bartender. "I was married for eight years," she says, "but I had to get rid of my husband. You see, I came home from work one day and there was blood on the toilet seat in the bathroom off the master bedroom, and blood on the rim, you know?"

The man gulps his cappuccino, but he keeps looking at her, sizing her up, she can see.

"And the thing was, I didn't have my period, so that was the end of Brent. I mean, he'd had some woman with him right there in my own bedroom and bathroom, and they were too sloppy to clean up the evidence."

The man looks embarrassed, but he is a fool, because instead of letting it go, keeping his mouth closed, he asks her nervously, "Any kids?"

"I had a daughter once, very briefly," she says, on a roll now. "She was stillborn, the cord wrapped around her neck, strangled."

Holly appears beside her and grabs her arm. "I'm sorry I'm late," she says, but she glares at Magda. She slams a five down on the bar as she pulls her sister away from it. "We're eating at Moose's, we can walk over if you're feeling okay." They walk along in silence.

"Didn't Mother ever tell you not to talk to strangers?" Holly says, her tone joking, but her eyes are hard and fixed on Magda's face. "You just can't resist jerking people around, can you? You're exactly like Whitey sometimes, you know that? You just thrive on making people squirm."

Chastened, Magda walks in lockstep with her sister to Moose's for lunch, silent. She looks up toward a yeasty group of cotton white clouds in the sky, but her glance falls upon a billboard advertisement of a long-distance telephone service, with letters as tall as men: "Somewhere in the world, there's someone you'd like to be able to call every single day," the ad proclaims.

She thinks for an instant, frozen in the moment, but she comes to the grim conclusion, No, there really *isn't*, there isn't anyone.

She is on her way to the blood bank again, walking there this time. The idea for the blood-letting had come to her from nowhere, a bit of whimsy really. She had suspected for a long time that the biological clocks that pop scientists claim women possess might be a reality. Women's bodies were spooky, she knew that. Hadn't she known each time within hours of conception that she was pregnant? The morning she hatched the idea of being a blood donor, she had been lying on the chaise longue in the garden drinking Snapple and listening to a CD of *La Boheme*, trying to get some sun on her legs, though she knew it could cause cancer of the skin. Maybe it was the music, Who knows what it was? but she suddenly thought of Carmen, the woman in the blood bank that day. And she knew she would go back there, right away, that in fact she would go there once a month. She looked at her calendar and saw that, yes, it had been exactly two months since the procedure, that her monthly cycle had been absent twice and that her body was sensing it. There is a macabre humor to it, is there not? she thinks — finding a way to restore harmony to her system, to let blood out, to foster life. In fact, as she goes up to the blood bank in the elevator, she recalls the rock group who used to wear T-shirts saying "CHOOSE LIFE." It had embarrassed her at the time, but now it sort of sends her, gives her juice.

Carmen isn't there when Magda enters the blood bank, but there is another genial woman wearing a pink smock and a pleasant smile. Magda tells her she would like to donate blood, that her blood type would be on file.

"Do you have a few minutes to spare?" the woman asks her. "We've got quite a crowd here today waiting to donate — a real run on the blood bank. You could say that business is great!"

For an instant, Magda is tempted to complete the sequence. She laughs, hears herself laugh, and feels a goofy, glamorous incandescence as blood surges to her head.

rapture

"Enjoy your trip to Las Vegas," the baggage tagger says, flashing her a lewd wink. He looks like Prince, she thinks, "the artist formerly known as Prince." Maggie loves this part: The curbside checking of bags is always her favorite moment at the beginning of a trip. Ever since she left Brent, being in airports has been a completely different experience from what it used to be. Her husband had always bought the tickets, carried the bags, tipped the cabbies, spoken with the desk clerks, while she stood at his side, looking her best. He looked after her well on trips — saying things like, "My wife would like to have a sandwich brought to her on the beach," or "Could you please bring my wife a martini, up, with an olive?" Now she arranges for her own drinks, her own snacks; she checks her bags at the curb like a grown-up.

The curbside checkers are often handsome and flirtatious. They tag the lady's tapestry-covered suitcases full of lace bras and net sacks of panty hose and say, "Enjoy your stay in Las Vegas" — or London or New York — with sly smiles they'd never given Brent when he checked the luggage.

When she thinks of Las Vegas, Maggie always thinks of Joan Didion, probably because of *Play It As It Lays*. She woke up this morning with a migraine she cannot shake, reinforcing the Didion connection. She does not look forward to being in Las Vegas in August with a headache. Before she left the house she put on sunglasses with "gray #4" lenses — so dark they appear black, and swallowed a small dose of ergot and a larger dose of codeine. In spite of the headache, she is exhilarated as she walks along. In an airport on the way to some-where, she always feels that Anything is possible; reality is suspended, everything is in flux. The plane could crash, she could fall in love, she could vomit during the flight, she could win thousands in a casino.

Normally, she would stop for a plain iced tea in the airport bar and decline the in-flight cocktail, knowing she has a tendency to come down with headaches on airplanes. This time, however, she already has a migraine and feels there's nothing to lose. She has preflight nerves and decides a cocktail is what is called for: In combination with the painkillers she has taken, the alcohol will allow her to sleep on the plane. She loves walking into airport bars alone and ordering a drink, acting like a businessman, privileged and bold. She enjoys the ap-praising looks she gets from the men who drink alone in airport bars, and the sidelong glances from the men there with their wives. She orders a daiquiri instead of a stronger drink, so the bartender won't think she is an alcoholic or a slut, remembering Brent's drunken mother as she does so. In an advanced stage of alcoholism, but pre-tending to be "just a social drinker," Brent's mother used to amuse them by the posturing she would go through when she went out to dinner with them. She would speak in a soft, high pitch when she or-dered from the waiter, disguising her whiskey voice. "I'll have one of those cute little drinks," she would say in the tiny, doll-like voice, very Blanche DuBois — "What are they called, Brent? A Russian some-thing?" she would ask, knowing full-well that it was a Black Russian and that it was as strong as a martini.

"Where you headed?" the barkeep asks her when he places the drink in front of her. "Las Vegas," she says. She knows not to call it "Vegas" — she learned this from the guide book she bought. She was grateful for the information, as she had already been trying on the sound of "Vegas" and had told the sales clerk in Loehmann's, "I'll need this filmy skirt for Vegas." Turns out it's just as uncool as saying Frisco. "I'm going to see Wayne Newton," she says to the bartender, and is offended when he doesn't seem to realize she is joking.

Maggie's friend Shay is the mayor of a ski resort town in the Rockies and will be in Las Vegas this week for some sort of conference of western states city administrators. Coincidentally, Maggie is scheduled to be there at the same time for a workshop titled "The Approaching Millennium and Its Effect on Film Journalism." The two women have not seen each other in five years and have decided to have a reunion while they're both in Las Vegas. Neither Shay nor Maggie has ever so much as bought a lottery ticket, so they find the idea of three days in Las Vegas acutely amusing. "What on earth will we *do* there in the evenings?" Maggie had asked Shay. "We can always go see Wayne Effing Newton," she replied.

She does sleep on the plane, only to wake in Las Vegas in the terminal phase of a migraine — the phase in which there is a feeling of terror and desperation, when everything seems polluted by a shattering nuclear light. What was I supposed to do? she wonders — cancel my trip this morning just because I felt a migraine coming on? Am I supposed to hunker down like a coward and whine, "I can't"? She also wonders why in hell the film journalism conference and the urban leaders conference have to be held in Las Vegas in the heat of August — is this someone's sick idea of a joke, or had someone's palm been liberally greased to make such absurd arrangements? The same guidebook that warned travelers against saying "Vegas" mentioned the Traveler's Aid Society. Apparently they provide dark quiet rooms in airports and conference centers for migraineurs in the throes of an attack. She does not have the presence of mind to seek such a quiet room, and instead lurches toward the line of taxis, vans, and limos at the curb in the sweltering heat. She chooses a van service, thinking it will have good air-conditioning and be cheaper than a taxi, probably worth the inconvenience of sharing a ride with strangers.

The temperature is 110 degrees in the shade as Maggie climbs into the van with five strangers, and she realizes immediately that the interior of the vehicle is not much cooler. A Japanese lady sits up front with the driver — an African American man who tells them his name is Kevin; Maggie sees a photo-i.d. clipped to the sun visor: Kevin Washington. In back are an older couple from Florida, two girls from Los Angeles who complain of a flight-from-hell, and a semitic-looking man with a New York accent who says he is from Coral Gables and that he has been coming to Las Vegas for decades. The latter wears checkered pants and is an obvious gambler—he quickly responds to each and every question the other passengers ask the driver, clearly an expert on Las Vegas. The driver cuts in to tell the passengers that just last night the new Planet Hollywood had opened inside Caesar's Palace. "George Bush was there for the opening," he tells them. The gambler says deadpan, "I'm very sorry to have missed seeing George Bush." Maggie is the only one who laughs appreciatively into the silence—she has recognized him as the liberal Democrat that a man from Coral Gables via New York was likely to be. He gives her a smile and they exchange a comradely look. She no longer feels like Joan Didion—she feels hot and irritable and drunk and the pain of the migraine is threatening to make her vomit.

"The air-conditioning doesn't seem to be working," she says to Kevin the driver.

"It's working," he insists, "but there are six of us heating up the air in here."

Recognizing the Blame-the-Victim tactic, she returns to silence. She catches a glimpse of Kevin's face in the rearview mirror and sees that she has annoyed him with her complaint; his mouth is a flaccid squiggle that turns down at each corner, a cold noodle left on a plate. She wonders why so many African American men are named Kevin these days—Why an Irish name? Every third basketball player on every NBA team is a black guy named Kevin. The travel glow that she had felt on the homeside of the trip has completely dissipated, and she gives in to a sad fantasy of Brent being there to deal with the driver and the doorman and the bellman, to say, "Please bring my wife an ice pack and some herb tea, and I'll need the extension for the hotel's physician."

Maggie's hotel is the last one on the van route and she is alone with the driver for the last few blocks of the ride. She has never liked being alone in a vehicle with a strange man, but chides herself for being old-ladyish. Kevin looks as if he pumps iron on weekends or takes ste-roids. In fact, as she looks at him more closely, she realizes that he looks like the body builder in the headlines last year who killed his blonde aerobic instructor girlfriend in a 'roid rage after she told him she'd slept with someone else. He had tossed her about like a rag doll and then stabbed her, but claimed he hadn't really meant to hurt her. She finds herself jiggling her foot nervously and is happy when the van pulls up in front of her hotel. She pulls out her wallet and extracts some of the one- and five-dollar bills she brought along for tips. She has always felt that it is good luck to tip everyone well on a trip, that it is a bit of shamanism to ensure a safe voyage out and back. She re-members Hemingway's Jake Barnes, who claimed a good tip was like insurance, assuring everyone would always be glad to see you again.

Kevin hops out and slides the van door open for her. To her embar-rassment, she cannot unhook the seat belt and struggles to get the metal hook out of its groove. She grapples fiercely with it for nearly twenty seconds, while Kevin stands there smiling. "I can't get out," she announces. "I'm afraid you're stuck with me." He laughs then, and she knows they are both envisioning driving around on the van's rounds for the next few hours with Maggie strapped in back like abandoned baggage.

"Allow me," says Kevin with a flourish, and places his massive dark hands near her lap; she can feel their heat as he tugs at the belt. "I'm surprised you can *breathe*!" he exclaims, and then pronounces that the belt is twisted several times over and has been fastened upside down. She smells the pomade in his glistening hair and knows he smells her perfume and perhaps even the Binaca she sprayed into her mouth just before she deplaned. She feels both seduced and menaced and sighs with relief when he releases her. "Thank you so much," she says, and hands him some discreetly folded bills which he acknowledges with a sweet smile and best wishes.

When Maggie follows the bellman into her hotel room, she sees that Shay is on the telephone, a glass of white wine in one hand and a cigarette in the other. "But in this case, we don't *want* the jacuzzi right next to the bed," Shay is saying into the phone, her voice a bit shrill. "It's not *appropriate*." She blows a kiss at Maggie, rolls her eyes, then points to the ceiling above the bed and grimaces. Maggie looks up and sees herself reflected in a mirror as large as the queen-sized bed: She looks tough in her dark glasses and has the pallor of someone who has not left the baccarat table for weeks except to go to the bathroom. Shay glimmers in the mirror, her white linen suit still fresh. "Yes, I'll expect to hear back from you right away," Shay says, cursing as she hangs up. To Maggie she says, "They gave us the honey-moon suite," and jabs her cigarette toward the bedside jacuzzi and again at the mirror on the ceiling. She and Maggie advance toward each other and air kiss, saying simultaneously, "You look exactly the same!"

In fact, Maggie notices Shay's crow's feet and she knows Shay couldn't miss her own jowls, and both of them now have uniformly mahogany hair with the reddish sheen that says dyed. Maggie lies down on the bed, on the opposite side from where Shay had been lying, her head hurting too much to unfasten the buckles on her T-strap pumps. "I'm sorry, Shay — I have a migraine," she mumbles.

"You never did travel well," Shay says. "Remember the time when you and Brent and Larry and I took my kids camping and you spent most of the time out behind the tent puking?"

"Yes, and then there was the time you guys had to drag me to that quack in Baja when I had dysentery." Though they both laugh, Maggie feels ashamed to be so feeble.

"Don't worry about it," Shay says quickly, "We'll just keep a low profile tonight and you'll feel better in the morning."

She is grateful to Shay for this and asks, trying not to whine, "Could you have room service bring me a martini? I'll wash some codeine down with it and maybe I can catch a few winks." After Shay calls for the drink, Maggie asks her to dig the sleep mask out of her overnight bag.

Shay laughs. "You're going to wash down pills with a martini, wearing a black mask over your eyes?" she says. "How von Bulow."

"Are we supposed to sleep together?" Maggie asks, thinking that's the last thing she needs right now, a woman in bed with her.

"Probably tonight we will. They don't expect to be able to get us another room until tomorrow afternoon." Shay says nothing more and Maggie realizes she has probably hurt her feelings. They sit quietly until the room-service waiter brings the martini for Maggie and another glass of wine and package of Virginia Slims for Shay.

Maggie sits up and takes off the black mask, and she and Shay clink glasses. "Downstairs in the lobby, I saw a photo on the wall of King Hussein at the White House," Maggie says. "I wonder why King Hussein — do you suppose he's a regular gambler here?" Shay shrugs, and Maggie says, "In the photo, he's so much tinier than the president — he looks like a miniature man or a big doll. It's funny — I just saw him on TV this morning — I caught the tail end of his speech at the White House." She sees both disinterest and lack of awareness on Shay's face, shining forth with a certain truculence. Maggie has a jolting suspicion that Shay may think she is talking about Saddam Hussein. *We've drifted too far apart,* she realizes, and wonders if the entire trip is doomed.

She awakens free of her headache, feeling fresh and happy. When she pulls off her sleep mask, Shay says, "Don't look up." When she does, she sees Shay and her mirrored on the ceiling, lying side by side together under the sheets. They laugh in unison, and Maggie murmurs, "Ah, the honeymoon suite."

Migraine has only one benefit, Maggie thinks, and that is how wonderful she feels when it has gone away. Trying to explain this to anyone is impossible — she has likened it to the cliché of someone banging his head savagely against a wall just because it feels so good when he stops, but this comes off sounding masochistic. In fact, the feeling of serenity and well-being — the complete and all-encompassing *lack* of pain — that comes after a migraine is analogous to the period of calm equanimity that Dostoyevsky wrote about having after epileptic seizures.

"Do you think we'll see any Elvis impersonators?" she asks.

"I've already seen six of them in full King regalia walking around the hotel," Shay says. "This just so happens to be the anniversary of his death—he died on August 16th, or so the bartender downstairs tells me. He said he remembers it vividly because he was in Rome at the time—he was sitting in a café and saw a newspaper with the headline 'ELVIS MORT'."

They had planned on breakfast buffets to save money, but instead they call room service for breakfast and a program guide. "Ask them to send up the *New York Times*," she says, and Shay asks "What for?" with a puzzled look. Maggie stifles the urge to snap, "So I can be informed," not wanting to revive the tension of the evening before. "I need to check something out," she answers, wondering if Shay has always been so provincial, and if she herself has always been so snappish and judgmental. One thing that has not changed is that they're both continually dieting, just as they were when they met twenty years ago. They're both still thin as pencils though they fret about their weight and Maggie has brought along a new panty-girdle. They eat grapefruit halves and dry wheat toast with their coffee, and suddenly Shay shrieks. "Oh my god! Wayne's back—that's what it says in the program guide. Wayne Newton came back to Vegas two days before he was scheduled to—we can go see him for a hoot."

Shay begins wheeling-and-dealing on the phone: arranging for transfer of their bags to the new room, lining up tickets for Wayne Newton and making an inquiry about the Star Impersonators show. She smokes and talks constantly, laughing pleasantly with everyone she talks to and blowing smoke around the room while Maggie lies inert on the opposite side of the bed, staring at her reflection on the ceiling. It occurs to Maggie that Shay is "the man" on this trip—the one who makes most of the decisions, does all the calling around, and takes care of the arrangements. Probably the room-service waiters assume they're in the honeymoon suite because they are a lesbian couple and that Maggie is the femme.

She wonders if she will really go to the morning seminar or if she should rent a car and go to Hoover Dam or if she should just find out what time Spago opens and go hang out. She realizes she does not have much stomach, suddenly, for the discussions about the effect of the approaching millennium on film journalism; she would rather make a vacation out of these few days away. She considers that per-haps she's having a depression, if she is more interested in seeing an aging pop singer or an Elvis impersonator than she is in a seminar in her chosen field. She can understand, though, why so many lowbrows keep seeing Dead Elvis walking around. She had forgiven Elvis every-thing the day he died on the bathroom floor at Graceland: the beach movies, "Love Me Tender," the bloated pop concert in Hawaii — everything. Elvis died the same day she had the first miscarriage — Brent had assumed she was sobbing about the baby, but it was the death of Elvis that had torn her apart.

The morning seminar turned out to be geared more toward film-makers than journalists, and Maggie had ducked out during the after-noon break and adjourned to Spago. She is to meet Shay there for dinner before the early Wayne Newton show. The restaurant is in "The Forum" section of Caesar's Palace; Maggie and Shay discovered early in the day that the Forum was the only place they could feel relaxed in Las Vegas. Everywhere else they went, there was too much noise, overwhelmingly bright lights, badly dressed people whose scanty clothing revealed their pasty-flabby bodies, some covered with embarrassing nets of coarse black hair. The Forum shops are indoors, in an artificial-outdoors environment. Puffy white clouds float by in the cerulean blue fake sky of the Forum, seemingly always at dusk. The temperature in the Forum never varies; it is always a comfortable seventy degrees, in spite of the blazing desert heat outside. Maggie figures it is probably the gurgling of the fountain and the dreamy mood of the omnipresent twilight that makes the Forum so soothing.

When she looks up to the sky, she sees handsome naked Roman statues looking down at her.

She wants to sit at one of the tables in front of the bar at Spago, adjacent to the Forum walkway, so she can watch the ebb and flow of pedestrians as if she were really in Rome. Even though it's still early, no empty tables remain. She feels like Brent's mother again — afraid of being judged a floozy for sitting at the bar, but she figures the conference badge on her dress gives her a veneer of respectability. She chooses a stool next to two grizzled old guys wearing meeting badges. They are talking animatedly about Rupert Murdoch and do not even glance up as she sits down.

Maggie's shoulder bag is too cumbersome to hold on her lap at the bar, so she lowers it to the floor after fishing out her wallet and the hardback Elvis biography — the one that had received good reviews in the *Times* just before Christmas. She had rented the *Viva Las Vegas* video last week to get in the mood for the trip, and that had put her in an Elvis mode. She is embarrassed to be seen reading an Elvis book like some trailer-park cretin, so she has removed the book's jacket. She knows she has at least an hour to kill before Shay shows up, but she does not wish to go back alone to their room. She orders a gin and tonic and opens to a page with a photo of young Elvis and Dewey Phillips walking down Beale Street. God, he was sultry when he was young, she thinks. People forget nowadays that Elvis was the closest thing we had to raw sex in those repressed times — the girls in his audiences fainted dead away not from lack of oxygen, but from sheer lust.

The gin and tonic cools and relaxes her and the Elvis bio is remarkably well written, so Maggie settles comfortably into reading at the bar. She is only marginally aware that the two old journalists have paid and gone and that a man by himself has taken the seat next to her. She does not glance up, nor does he say anything to her. He has a nice voice when he orders a Beck's, but she turns slightly away from him as she continues to read. Suddenly the bartender says, "Excuse me, Miss — " and points to a red-headed man at the far end of the bar —

"the gentleman from Looziana sends you this with his regards," and places another g&t in front of her. It has been years since someone has sent her a drink in a bar; she realizes in a bit of a panic that she does not really know the protocol. Impulsively she turns to the man sitting next to her and blurts out, "Will I be compromised if I accept this drink?"

"Compromised?" he looks appraisingly at her, and as she sees his face for the first time, she observes that he is youngish and handsome. What are the odds, she wonders, of having a handsome guy sit right next to you, particularly at the same moment some other guy is sending you a cocktail? "I don't think I've heard anyone actually use the word compromised like that before," he responds. He looks over toward the gentleman from Looziana, who is wearing an LSU sweatshirt and grinning their way.

"If I drink this, does it mean I'm allowing him to make a pass at me?" She stares at the fresh gin and tonic, afraid to look over at the donor.

"Oh hell, just drink it," the good looking guy says, "and shine him on."

She and the guy laugh together and she takes a sip from the drink; she tries not to stare, but his convention badge says "Duncan Gordon" — he's attending the same conference she's supposed to be going to. She returns to the Elvis biography, feeling uneasy now about the red-haired LSU guy watching her read at the bar. Duncan asks her what she's reading. She likes him for not asking her until she had spoken to him first; she cannot abide a pushy guy. There's no way out of telling him that she's reading an Elvis book. "The new Elvis bio," she admits, "It received good reviews. I took the dust jacket off — I was embarrassed . . ."

He laughs. "I just read it myself. I teach a course on popular culture at the New School." He tells her the *Mystery Train* chapter is the best and asks her if she's read a book by the same name.

She cannot help it; she sneaks a look at his hand and sees that he wears a wedding ring. So much the better; maybe he won't make a pass at her, and if he does she can pretend to be shocked because he's married. There will be less chance of their drinking too much and pretending to fall in love.

She's in the middle of asking him about *Mystery Train* when she hears a shrill beeping coming from her purse. "I have to get that," she says, knowing it could only be Shay, who had forced one of the hotel's conventioneer beepers on Maggie in case she had to track her down. She feels a rush of relief when Duncan bends down to get her purse for her — she hates the kind of man who will just sit by and watch a woman struggle. "Thank you so much," she says, and fishes out the beeper. She laughs at the 666 read-out that appears on the screen and says, "It's my friend — I have to go call her." Before she can pay and leave, Duncan says, "I'll watch your purse," and pulls it to his lap. At the same moment, he signals the bartender for another round. It's been decided for her; she will call Shay and then come back and talk some more with this stranger.

"Our dinner plans are screwed," Shay tells her when she calls her back. "I'm stuck having dinner with some horse's-ass city manager from Montana — there's no way out of it. I'm going to have to meet you at the Wayne Newton show — I'll be right in front about fifteen minutes early — please don't be mad."

"It's OK," she tells Shay. "I'll see you there later." As she walks back into Spago, she feels as if fortune has smiled on her. She is free to talk with Duncan for hours if she pleases, but has a perfect excuse to duck out in case he puts the moves on her.

It is only as she walks across the restaurant toward the bar that she realizes this Duncan guy looks very much the way her ex-husband looked when she met him. She is surprised to find herself entering into a flirtation with a man who looks like the one who wrecked her life, but she cannot ignore the fact that he looks very much like Brent — bearded and tweedy with a boyish face and wide gray eyes. In fact, if anyone from home saw her with this man, they might first assume she was with Brent. Maggie tends to discount psychological theories, but the truth is that Brent was just like her father, and that each man she has been with since the divorce has been a hybrid of her father and Brent; she has to wonder if all her choices are made in a fatefully subliminal manner. When she sits down, she sees a fresh gin and tonic on her place at the bar and a cocktail napkin with a note scrawled on it. "Please come over and talk to me before you leave," it says, signed, "Chuck (Louisiana)." She looks over at the redhead who sent her a drink and he makes the motion of tipping an imaginary hat at her; she flushes and looks away.

"Don't worry — this drink isn't from that guy," Duncan tells her, handing her another gin and tonic, and she thanks him.

"I'm drinking too much, though," she says to Duncan, and points at the glasses lined up in front of her. "If I stay any longer, I'd better switch to Perrier." In fact, she is beginning to feel the euphoric rush just verging on dizziness that sets in when she makes the mistake of drinking without food. Or maybe it is just giddiness at having two men plying her with drinks at one time.

Duncan is a film critic, it turns out, so rather naturally they begin talking about movies. They had both been to the film festivals at Telluride and Sundance and they begin swapping stories about whom they'd met and which films they'd seen, and they both gesture a lot. She touches his arm a couple of times when she becomes excited about a particular film or another, and her fingertips feel singed on contact with the genteel tweed — she imagines she sees sparks.

Duncan had talked to Robert Altman at Telluride and she had seen Kurosawa at Sundance and they argue over who's usually right, Siskel or Ebert, and she notices that the critic's hair is curly, though not as curly as Brent's, and she blushes when she bites into the lime wedge because it seems such a sensual thing to do.

"Did you see *The Rapture* when you were at Telluride?" she asks him. This is a litmus test — the film is one that people either really hate or really love; if he doesn't like it, doesn't *get* it, they aren't on the same wavelength, no matter that he's attractive as hell.

"I loved it," he says. "I liked it for the chances it took — the audience didn't know what to make of it."

She says, "I liked it for the creepy holy feeling it gave me."

"Is that why you came to Las Vegas?" he asks, lighting a cigarette and looking away.

"What do you mean?" she asks, thinking Oh Christ, what *does* he mean?

"The woman in the film had a vision that she needed to go to the desert to find God—well, you've come to the desert." He smiles and she knows he's OK.

"The film also claimed you can go to heaven without dying," she says.

"I don't think you'll find God in Spago," Duncan says, "but you can *wait* for him here. That's another thing I liked about *The Rapture*—that the woman waited for God in the desert and he didn't come—I felt there was some sort of parallel there with *Waiting for Godot*, didn't you?"

She loves him now, there's nothing to be done for it. "I did think of *Godot!*" she says. "But you know what someone in *The Rapture* said: 'Only the humble hear the voice of God.'"

He says they're probably out of luck, in that case, and they both begin to be more than half drunk, and the conversation zips and zags while they both wave their arms and he smokes cigarettes and they order more cocktails and she completely forgets about Shay and Wayne Newton. She thinks again, as she has before, that she holds a profound double-standard when it comes to cigarettes: When Shay or her sister, Holly, smokes, she is annoyed, but when a man smokes she finds it inherently sexy.

"Have you seen any of those car bumper stickers that say 'BEWARE OF RAPTURE—CAR MAY BECOME DRIVERLESS'?" he asks.

They both laugh and scoff and talk about what the guy in the *Times* said about *The Rapture* and Duncan says of the ascension scene, "I can't say that I've ever had a moment quite like *that* in my life," and she answers without hesitation, "*I* have." She hopes he won't ask her what she means and he doesn't, but there's a moment when they look at each other for a long time and she senses the presence of a wind tunnel, ready to whoosh them both in. She chooses a distancing-maneuver and asks, "Where's your wife?"

"She's not with me this time," he responds, not missing a beat. Five seconds of silence intervene before he says, "She said she was too busy to come, but she has another agenda." His voice is blasé but she sees an ill-disguised burst of pain in his eyes before he takes another casual sip from his beer.

"A beau?" she asks.

His laughter is urbane but bitter, a little machine-gun rat-a-tat ha-ha. "You could say that."

"I have to go soon. I'm going to see Wayne Newton."

"Say it ain't so," he says. "Wayne Newton — who'd have thought you'd be capable of something like that?" Then pointing at her badge, "Where's *Mister* Portman?"

"He betrayed me," she says. "That's all there is to tell, except that we've been divorced for three years."

She watches him watching her and for a second she thinks, Maybe this is it. She has been waiting, waiting since the day she discovered Brent's infidelity. Cold comfort and a few cold kisses have come her way, but three years have just leaked away, leeching the marrow out of her bones. She sees something in this Duncan's eyes: suffering? a question?

"You're different," he says.

She doesn't bother to ask what he means, comes back to her senses and thinks, *You're* not — you'll make a pass at me now. Perhaps he takes her silence as a sign she has fallen for the set-up, for he goes on to say, "How long are you going to be here?"

The panic has come down on her by then, and her heart pounds so hard it feels as if it swells up to the size of a beefsteak, hot and pulsing in her breast. She is looking at his lips, lush and reddish, but she no longer listens to what he says; the decision has been made — she'll adjourn to the ladies' room and never come back.

She meets Shay at the Sands, but she is having second thoughts. "I wonder why we're doing this," she says to Shay. "I think we're getting too old for high camp, and I think the show's a bit pricey for just campiness value."

"Don't be a grump," Shay says. "How can we go to Las Vegas without seeing Wayne Newton? — we can tell our grandchildren about it after Wayne's dead."

Shay seems to have forgotten that Maggie will have no grandchildren, but Maggie does not remind her. "Arsenio Hall likes him," she says instead. "He said on television that he was surprised when he saw Wayne's show — he said he was really a cool brother and that his show had it goin' on." She does not tell Shay that Newton had given Arsenio an Arabian horse as a token of his friendship, and that this might have earned him a plug on TV.

The early show is a mistake. The blue-rinse crowd is out in full force, though Maggie supposes the late show will have plenty of them as well. Newton's show depresses her and Shay — there is no high camp here at all. The audience is studded with shills: a little girl named "Angel" who comes up to the stage and gives him a flower; a man who jumps to his feet and calls out boisterous compliments to Newton; an old lady who joins him in a song, singing into the microphone in perfect harmony, knowing every word. But things grow worse: Newton begins to make Indian jokes. The second time he calls himself "a dumb Indian," Shay turns to Maggie and says, "I didn't know he was an Indian, but this is appalling."

Shay still knows the score, after all, Maggie thinks. The two of them sit dejected and silent while Newton makes self-deprecatory Native American jokes, pandering to the racism of the crowd. Maggie watches a horsey elderly man bite down on the pineapple spear in his mai tai and thinks of the lime she bit into earlier that day — at the same instant, she imagines Duncan biting down hard on the tender flesh near her shoulder blade, his teeth white and sharp, drawing blood. She shakes her head to get the image out. Shay sees her and nods, assuming she's shaking her head over Wayne Newton. Just as he makes a firewater joke, they give each other the high-sign and get up to leave.

A sweet-faced old maître d' with a silver toupee follows them with a wounded expression. "You don't like the show?" he asks, clearly taking it personally. They do not have the heart to tell him, and Shay says, "We think maybe we're, you know, perhaps a bit *wrong* for this particular show."

Maggie wakes up to the sound of a badly played trumpet coming from the next room over.

"Are you awake?" Shay whispers.

"Yes, Herb Alpert Junior woke me." Maggie sits up and switches on the lamp by her bedside. "Is there any Perrier left?"

Shay is already lighting up a Slim, and she frowns. "I'm thirsty, too, but it's the other kind of thirst — the kind that cries out for a bowl of sherbet, a tall 7-Up and a side of vodka to fend off the hangover that's on the way." She reaches for the phone.

"Can we really get room service at three in the morning?" Maggie asks.

"This is Las Vegas," Shay reminds her.

She listens to her order two bowls of sherbet, two diet 7-Ups and two shots of Skyy. In their new room, there are no mirrors above their two double beds, and the beds are far enough apart so that Shay's chain-smoking is not as irritating as it could be, though the air has become rank. Maggie is not as tolerant of Shay's reading material; she has bought a copy of the *National Enquirer* and whips it out as they wait for room service. A perfect example of the mentality of our public servants, Maggie thinks — Shay acted baffled when I ordered the *Times* but sits here shamelessly reading a tabloid; she'll probably go far in politics, could be the next token female vice-presidential nominee. Shay disarms her, however, with a raucous blast of laughter.

"Quote," Shay says, "'Regis wanted to have sex with me on his wedding anniversary.' I wonder if that's Kathie Lee or someone else." She thumbs rapidly through the newspaper.

"Who's Regis?" Maggie asks, but doesn't really listen to Shay's response. She is thinking of her tenth wedding anniversary, when she'd noticed a sheepish look on Brent's face as they cut the St. Honore cake that was a twin to the one they'd cut on their wedding day. He knew what she had yet to find out: He had been in bed with another woman that very afternoon.

"Come in!" they chime when the waiter knocks, not wishing to get up in their revealing nighties, Shay's pink silk and Maggie's opaque mint-green lisle. Like many of the hotel staff, the young man is devastatingly handsome and has a chic haircut; Maggie wonders if he might be a part-time actor or singer. He rolls the table right up in between their beds and serves them in their bedclothes with a flourish, spooning fresh berries atop the sherbet, tumbling the 7-Up over tall glasses of ice. "Our neighbor's serenade woke us up," Maggie says. "We didn't know if you'd come at three o'clock in the morning."

"Oh, this is our busiest time of the day, Ladies," he says. "Here you can have *anything*, anything you want, twenty-four hours a day."

"Wow," Shay whispers, and the room is quiet for a few moments. Maggie thinks about the truth: She can have *nothing* that she wants, twenty-four hours a day, here or at home, nada.

"Hair of the dog?" the waiter asks, gesturing toward the chilled vodka on the tray.

They laugh in unison and blush when they notice the waiter glancing at their bosoms. Maggie is considering that maybe this is what it has come to: Maybe for the rest of her life room-service waiters will be the only men who will serve her in bed. Shay takes a sip of the vodka and says, "Sweet Jesus that's good." After the waiter leaves, she asks Maggie, "Where were you when I paged you?"

"Spago. I met a guy."

"Did you like him?"

"Married guy, looked just like Brent. Started to make a pass at me."

"Were you flattered, or did it make you feel like two cents?" Shay asks.

"Both. I bailed on him."

"What happened?"

"First we talked about a movie we both liked," Maggie says, "and we got a bit tanked-up, actually. Did you see *The Rapture*?"

"No, what is it?"

Maggie doesn't want to get into the whole thing with Shay and tries to think of a way to describe the premise of the rapture phenomenon. "Well," she says, "there are some religious fanatics who think that those who are supposedly saved can be taken bodily into heaven while they're still alive."

Shay gives a short barking laugh and lights another cigarette and Maggie goes on, "They say that their bodies will be transformed into spirits and they'll be caught up in the clouds to meet God."

"And you talked about *that* with the guy you drank with in Spago?"

"No, we talked about the movie about it, and we talked about other things, and there was a, you know, a buzz between us, a sort of rush or pull."

"And then?"

"God, Shay," she says. "Why fall for a married man, and why fall for a married man in a bar in Las Vegas for goodness sake? I might as well just stab myself in the heart."

"A brief romance never killed anyone, Magdalena," Shay says. She turns on the television and flips to a repeat of the late-night news. A man has been found dead in an abandoned house outside of Las Vegas.

"There's a weird twist to this story, folks," says the well-coiffed anchorman. "Seems the deceased man lived in that very house forty years ago."

Shay turns up the volume, and she and Maggie lie silently, staring at the screen.

"The forty-five-year-old man had been in the hospital with an Alzheimer-like disease," the anchor says, "but he left the hospital without permission and somehow managed to get himself across town, still wearing hospital slippers. He found the ruined shell of the family home he lived in as a youth," he says, "and there his body was found Sunday in the debris of a home ravaged by thieves and time."

Maggie had gone back to her old home once, too. "No-Fault Divorce" turned out to be one more bad joke for females — what it really meant was that the divorce was never the man's fault anymore. In spite of Brent's adultery, she could not have him thrown out of the house. She had to leave Brent and move to a rented condo with cottage-cheese ceilings and grotesque avocado shag carpet while she waited for the divorce to go through. Brent kicked back in their two-storey house, comfy amongst the Persian carpets and the eclectic furnishings they'd chosen together over the years. Her former neighbors had told her that Brent entertained his girlfriends there in Maggie's absence, barbecuing marinated chicken breasts out on the patio while the young women drank wine coolers in their bikinis. The house had to be sold when the divorce went through — she and Brent had never been good with money.

She had gone back there one day, almost as if on automatic pilot. Probably she had been in a mild state of shock; she had just left her doctor's office and had driven to her former house rather than to the condo. The doctor had told her that day that she would have to have her womb removed, that there was really no choice, and she had found herself mumbling crazily as she drove away from the medical building, incoherent and dazed. Until that day, she had clung to the gossamer hope that maybe some day there would be a family, that maybe it wasn't too late.

Stunned to discover herself turning into the street where they used to live, Maggie's first reaction had been to make a U-turn and speed away, but she changed her mind. "I'll just do a fly-by," she had said aloud, aware by then that she was on the verge of hysteria. Just by chance, roll of the dice, the new family were unpacking groceries from their Volvo and carrying them onto the porch. The house, painted white now, still had the Austrian shade Maggie had chosen in the up-stairs bedroom window. "A nice family," she said to herself, "happy." The wife had pink hair and wore tiger-striped leggings; the husband was bald and homely. She actually heard him as she drove by, heard him say in a warbly voice, "Let me help you with that, honey," and she heard the two boys, chubby and pie faced like their mother, arguing in a brotherly manner: *I did not!* blah blah. And she had to wonder: What had Brent's and her good looks and excellent taste actually done for them? All she could think was, I missed the goddam boat.

Shay has switched the channel to old concert footage of Elvis. The vodka has evidently put her in a talking mood, so she mutes the sound as soon as she notices Maggie's attention riveting upon Elvis. "Train I ri-ide," is all Maggie catches before the sound goes off, but she knows her Elvis trivia well enough to remember the words to "Mystery Train." She knocks back the Skyy vodka in one quick motion the way she had noticed gamblers doing in the casino, and there is an instantaneous pay-off—her head reels and she feels a lifting sensation, a pulling upward of her mood and spirit, almost of her body from the bed. But something else happens, then, more than the vodka: As she watches Elvis gyrate, sees the painful sexual grimace on his face as he sings, he seems to grow larger on the screen, to shimmer the way things do before a migraine attack. She hears Shay talking, something about seeing Cher in the lobby, her voice fading to a dull buzz in Maggie's ears. He rises out of the screen in his dazzling white King suit with the stiff high collar, and she feels herself levitating from the bed like a magician's assistant in her filmy gown, hears a rushing sound as she and Elvis lift through the roof in rapture.

zoe

skin and bone

Zoe began having her face peeled shortly after her husband left her. She had seen a full-page advertisement in a local magazine for a female dermatologist who specialized in cosmetic skin care and collagen injections. She knew the time had come for that sort of thing and telephoned for an appointment.

Her new dermatologist, Dr. Allen, was a pretty blonde woman with an office in a remodeled Victorian house. Zoe liked the suite much more than that of the male skin doctor she had visited for an uncharacteristic breakout of acne. The skin man had worn a starchy white lab coat and a condescending expression; he cruelly scraped her face with some sort of instrument, causing her to bleat slightly; and he told her to never again use the nightcream she had used for eight years. She hated his guts.

When Zoe first walked into Dr. Allen's office, the receptionist offered her an apple and gave her some literature about collagen injections for wrinkles and scars. Dr. Allen's dachshund trotted freely through the waiting room and hall. The secretary called the dog "Strudel."

"Oh, you're a pretty one," Dr. Allen said after the facial-cleansing woman removed all of Zoe's makeup and steamed her face.

"Not really," Zoe protested, thinking, If I'm so pretty, why did Dan leave me for another woman?

"What Sherry did to you today," Dr. Allen explained, "was to totally clean up your face and then apply a firming mask. Now I'll get rid of some of those broken blood vessels around your nose, and then we'll do a chemical peel. You will be simply glowing from the peel when you leave, and tomorrow you will look even better. The next day, though, your face will turn slightly brownish in spots and then the top layer of your skin will peel off and you will look gorgeous."

"Oh, good," Zoe responded listlessly. "Gorgeous" was what Dan had called Cindy, the woman he lived with now.

"We'll give you a collagen test today, just to make certain you're not allergic," the glamorous physician continued. "My idea would be to fill those frown lines on your forehead with collagen, and also the lines beneath your eyes and the small ones on the side of your mouth. Then you would be perfect."

"Fill my frown lines?" Zoe asked. "Oh, no — I might look vacuous, then. I have to have some signs of character on my face."

"Well, whatever you think," Dr. Allen said. Then, "Are you married?"

"No," Zoe confessed. "I mean, I am, legally, but actually my husband has left me and is living with some girl."

"My husband left me, too!" the doctor announced. She lowered her voice, saying, "Look, I'll tell you everything you need to do to find men."

"I don't want to meet men," answered Zoe, shocked, but the doctor ignored her.

"First, you join the City Club. God, do you meet the men there. They have tennis, saunas, exercise classes, you name it, and everyone who goes there is young and well heeled. I meet tons of men there."

"I'm really not very athletic," Zoe said. "And, a little short on money since my husband left."

"Do you have a dog?" the doctor asked.

"Yes, a harlequin Great Dane."

"You have it made, then. All you do is go down to Union Street on the weekends with your beautiful face and your beautiful dog, and you'll have men flocking to you. I do it all the time with Strudel."

"Well, actually, I'm sort of going out with a man now, anyway," Zoe said, feeling uncomfortable. Having a lover seemed unsuitable and strange; she could not feel at ease about sleeping with any man but her husband.

"What's the boyfriend like?" the doctor wanted to know. "Is he as good or better than your husband? You can't backslide, you know."

This remark convinced Zoe that she need not worry about saying anything inappropriate, so she told Dr. Allen, "Well, he's a bit young, he smokes heavily, and he's usually broke. And when he is broke, sometimes he steals the Sunday paper off the porches of houses where it looks as if the owners are away."

"Good grief!" exclaimed Dr. Allen. "I don't think he's what you need."

"No, but he has a tiny waist and curly black hair," Zoe said, blushing a bit. She recalled the way Guy smiled at her the day she met him, only a few weeks ago. She had been wearing very dark glasses to hide her tear-ravaged eyes, and stumbled over Guy's foot as she boarded the city bus on the way to work.

"What about your husband?"

"He has a small waist, too, and wavy auburn hair."

"No! I mean what does he *do*?" the doctor demanded.

"He's in advertising," Zoe told her.

"He probably makes lots of money. Any chance of getting him back from the woman he's living with?"

"Who knows?" Zoe sighed. The doctor was daubing her face with something that burned.

"What do you do?" Dr. Allen asked.

"I do some free-lance graphics; I don't make a lot of money, if that's what you mean."

"No kids?"

"No kids," she said, wondering when her face would stop hurting.

"Thank god for that."

Oh, yes, thank god I have no one at all in the world, Zoe thought, but said nothing.

"This will give you a light peel," the doctor told her. "Next time we'll do a stronger one."

As Zoe rose to leave, the doctor unexpectedly said, "God, I bet you look great in a bathing suit. I never looked good in a bathing suit a day in my life. I'll see you in three weeks. Don't drink too much when you feel depressed and make sure you have a good attorney in case your husband tries to put the screws to you financially."

"Thank you," Zoe said weakly, her face stinging from the chemicals. She wondered if she would really return in three weeks.

Walking to the streetcar station, she saw a man carrying a red carnation leap out of a taxi and lunge at a flower vendor in front of a Union Square hotel. The taxi waited, engine running, while the irate man dressed down the flower vendor.

"I pay one dollar for one damned carnation, and you take it from a secret stash of half-dead carnations and wrap it up so I don't notice how ratty it is until I unwrap it at my office! You son of a bitch, that is GREEDY!" Then he gave the flower vendor the finger, hand raised high, thrusting at the air with his obscene gesture.

She had begun to notice that these gestures appeared in clusters. She wondered if it had something to do with phases of the moon. Just the evening before, she had dined in a trendy restaurant with her friend Caitlin, and it had happened there, too. She and Caitlin were sipping daiquiris before ordering dinner, and the woman at the table next to them sprang to her feet and screamed at her escort, "I nevah want to see you again in mah entire life!" and stiffly extended her middle finger at her companion as she stormed out. "How incongruous," Caitlin said.

The previous morning, Zoe had pulled out of a parking space without looking, and a man driving by had swerved to avoid her. He flipped her off after laying on his horn. He wore one earring and his car wore a bumper sticker saying, "I ♡ DICK."

She guessed no one would do this again for many weeks, and then it would start up again, occurring once or twice daily.

"Hey, Miss America, got any spare change?" a wino asked her as she passed through Union Square. She smirked slightly and walked on more rapidly. Miss America? Well, perhaps the peel was beginning to work, already.

She read the newspaper on the streetcar on the way home. The Saturday paper was always very strange, she thought. It was as if they saved up all the weird stories for the Saturday paper because there was no real news on Saturday.

On the front page was a headline, "MYSTERY SLAYING IN POSH HOME." Incredibly, her former orthodontist and his wife had been bludgeoned to death, and all signs pointed to their son being the murderer. She thought of all the hours she had spent in the orthodontist's office when she wore braces on her teeth, and then frowned when she thought of the man being battered to death. His body had been found in a reclining chair with a bathrobe draped loosely around it. She was surprised to realize this was the one story she had little reaction to. What interested her more was the story directly above it: "ARAB ADMIRER KEEPS LUCY A CARROT-TOP."

It seemed that Lucille Ball had bought her last fifty-pound bag of pure Egyptian henna twenty years before, thinking it would last the rest of her life. Now, she was seventy-two and running out of henna, and the type she needed was no longer imported into the United States. Lucy said the only henna she could get in the United States would turn her hair green. A Jordanian man read about Lucy's problem in an international magazine and sent her a bag of henna as a gift. He attached a note saying, "I am glad to send the henna for Mrs. Lucy and hope she will consume it during her happy and long life and I promise to send more to Mrs. Lucy in future." Zoe liked that. "The kindness of strangers."

Two blocks before her stop, she came to the back page of the paper. "CHIMP JUMPS ON CYCLE, MAULS BIKER," she read. "A 49-year-old biker attacked by a 4-foot-tall chimpanzee who hopped on his motorcycle during a traffic jam says he was hurting too much at the time to get scared."

I know how you feel, old buddy, Zoe thought, but she heard herself laughing aloud with a malicious tone that frightened her.

She began hitting parked cars again. Two days after Dan left, she had hit a Nissan Sentra parked to her right when she was backing out of a traffic space. When she heard the crunching metal, she panicked, her first thought being that she had to escape from the maimed car. The Sentra was brand new and must be well insured, she guessed. She was the one who was broke and had a heap for a car and no collision insurance. She knew the Valium she was taking was probably what had caused her accident — that and the fact that she had not slept more than two hours either of the nights since her husband had slammed the door behind him after calling her a "glutinous mass of raw emotion and quivering nerves." She stepped frantically on the accelerator and twisted the steering wheel of her Volkswagen, trying to disentangle her car from the Japanese one, but the noise only became louder and more hideously menacing. Putting the car into reverse, she was able only to drag the Sentra along with her for a few feet, but not able to break free and drive off. Furiously, she jockeyed the car forward and then back until with one last metallic shriek, her car pulled free of the other one. Sobbing, she drove away as fast as she could, hoping no one was taking down her license number. When she told her psychiatrist about it, he said, "It's odd that you seem to feel no remorse."

"I have no remorse at all — none," she lied, dry eyed.

Months later, the wrecks began again. First, she nicked the bumper of a van in the parking lot in front of the grocery, but the van was already banged up and no one saw her, so she was not upset. She thought coolly, I wonder why I'm crashing again? Then, only a few days later, she rammed a lime-green Lincoln Continental in the large downtown garage where she often parked. Looking in her rearview mirror, she realized at once that she had been observed by two persons. An elderly woman stood by the elevators, and an Asian man with a camera hanging from his neck had just stepped from a rental car. There is no way I can pay for body work, she thought. She tried to look confident and strode briskly to the stairwell, hoping that nothing would happen to her. She had a quick, crazy thought that maybe she would fall in love with the policeman who came to arrest her. Her mother had always told her to just approach any policeman if she were ever lost or in trouble. Well, she was both.

She was on her way to see Dr. Allen again, and she considered that while being peeled she might tell her about the hit-and-run. She sensed that Dr. Allen was on the verge of hysteria about her own impending divorce and was now stimulated only by the shocking and bizarre. Perhaps the doctor, too, had lost her sense of what was kind and right and seemly. Perhaps she mutilated parked cars and laughed cruelly when motorcyclists were mauled by monkeys.

"How was your peel?" Dr. Allen asked Zoe while her face was being steamed.

"Fine. I didn't turn very brown, and only my nose peeled really visibly." The steam was soothing; she felt as if she might fall asleep. She realized she was looking forward to having the top layer of her face burned off again. Once the pain stopped, the tingling would feel pleasant. The chemicals were like a slap in the face, a respite from the stuporous state she had been in for months.

"I'll tell you," Dr. Allen said, "I don't care what anyone says. . . what men really want in a woman is looks. I don't care how smart you are, what a great personality you have — what men want is a pretty face."

Zoe murmured, "Mmm," in neither agreement nor dissent.

"Men love skin," she continued. "They love it. How are things going with you and your husband?"

"He's still A.W.O.L.," she responded, feeling strange about having a conversation while lying down with pads over her eyes. Everything she said seemed overemphasized, as if she were shouting into a tunnel. "Yesterday, he came over to pick up his scuba diving gear, and he told me really cheerfully that he had never realized how much his entire family always hated me." She forced a laugh.

"Good riddance to all of them," Dr. Allen said. I could never tell you how glad I am to be rid of my in-laws. Have you decided about the collagen?"

"Not yet," she answered. She could not tell the doctor that she would feel strange about having a plastic face. She feared the collagen might shift around as silicone implants sometimes did, and her face become distorted. She imagined being "perfect" for a period of time after the injections, and then waking up one morning to see her face rutted, hideous hollows and lumps disfiguring it. She felt superstitious about trying to become beautiful; it was too much like the fairy tale about the three wishes. She did not want to end up with a sausage on her nose like the man who wished foolishly in the tale.

Before she left the office, she inadvertently delighted Dr. Allen by telling her that she and Guy were going to a performance that evening by a woman who screams into a microphone on stage, acting as if she is possessed. Walking down the hall to the elevator, she heard Dr. Allen's silvery laugh as she said to her assistant, "Zoe is such a character — can you imagine going out on a date to watch a woman get up and scream?"

Alone in the elevator, Zoe's face flamed from the latest round of chemicals.

She and Guy drank entirely too much wine before the screaming performance, and during the brief intermission they each gulped two more glasses in the lobby.

"Actually, the first minute or two were very intriguing," Guy said.

Zoe responded, "I liked her dress." The performer wore a skin-tight, black-sequined evening gown and demonic eye makeup. The first piece she screamed was entitled, "Wild Women with Steak Knives," amusing Zoe enough to make her save the program. When they left the small theater and realized they were nearly staggering, she suggested that perhaps they should leave the car there and take a cab back to her house. Guy whistled at a cab driving quickly past them, but the driver gave them the finger and continued speeding away.

"There must be a pattern, somewhere," Zoe slurred as they lurched into her lover's old Chevy.

She awoke at five o'clock in the morning, hearing the garbage men trashing the driveway. Guy, whom she had known less than a month, was lying exactly where Dan had slept for six years. Her husband. Dan. She felt unable to breathe, felt as if there were something crushing her downward through the mattress, and told herself it was only a hangover. She began weeping, awakening Guy.

"What's wrong, babe?" he asked in a soft, sleepy voice.

"It's my orthodontist," she said. "He's dead."

jump!

Zoe had been reading in bed, but stopped to stare at the wall. When she picked the book up again, she did not realize the book was upside down. Seeing the backwards and upside down printing on the page, she panicked for a second. The words looked foreign, and she was instantly disoriented, thought, This is not English! Where am I?

She knew it was only what she had begun to call "the 3 A.M. syndrome," and went to the kitchen for a glass of milk and some vitamin C caplets. The light was on in the house behind her apartment building, and she wondered if the couple there had stayed up late or risen early. The pair did not exist for her during three-quarters of the year, but in fall the green leaves and yellow plums disappeared from the trees outside her kitchen window and the rooms in the house became glaringly visible to Zoe. She often saw the couple eating meals at their kitchen table, the woman sometimes wearing a slip — Zoe thought of it as "the rayon slip" — fat and shameless. She was proud that at least she sat at her own table properly dressed and ate nice steaks or fresh fish by candlelight. At the very least, she ate frozen dinners on bone china. She vowed to buy a window shade, or to ask the landlord to do so.

She took the milk back to her bedroom with her and picked up the book again, thinking she would read for another fifteen minutes and then try to go to sleep. She was glad that Ian, her business partner, would open the office and that she would not have to go in before ten o'clock.

The telephone rang, surprising her. She assumed at first that it was "the Joyboy," as she termed the freak who had been telephoning her anonymously for months, talking about undergarments. But it was not the Joyboy — it was a young attorney she had met at a party a week before.

"It's Mark, from Caitlin's party — do you remember me?" he asked, sounding polite despite the rudeness of his timing.

"Yes, but . . ." she responded.

"You told Fritz Beecham — I heard you — that you are always awake at three — that you drink milk and take drugs and read biographies," the man said.

"Not drugs," she said. "Vitamins." She noticed a slender line of black ants on the quilt. "Nonfiction. Not particularly biographies." She brushed two or three ants off the mound her legs made under the bed quilt — there had been a problem with ants since summer — and killed the one crawling on her wrist.

He told her he had looked her name up in the telephone directory after Caitlin's party, that he had circled it with a red Magic Marker and had thought of her all week.

"I'd love to take you to dinner Saturday — will you go?" he asked.

She felt there was some sort of mistake. The fellow was thirteen years younger than she, barely old enough to be an attorney. She had asked him at the party if he had really already passed the bar. She ignored his invitation, said, "Do you know how to get rid of ants?"

"You have to kill the queen," he said with a certain authority.

She wanted to ask him how she could tell which one was the queen, but she did not. She thanked him for his advice and wrote down the telephone number he gave her, saying she would have to think about dinner.

She knew she would never call the man. She knew, even in the midst of 3 A.M. syndrome, that she would not telephone him, but would instead buy a Weight Watchers frozen pizza Saturday evening to heat for dinner and that she would eat it alone.

Turning out the bedside lamp, she wondered about the Weight

Watchers pizzas. In the Park 'N Shop, she had never seen anyone except other slim women buying the dinners. She could not decide whether the women were slim because they lost weight eating the dinners or if they were all chronically thin women exercising caution. She could not relate this phenomenon to the one she had noticed in the health food store. It seemed to be a case of opposites. The people in the health food store pushed carts full of organically grown vegetables, whole-grain everything, and bottles of acidophilus, but they had acne on their sallow skin. The hair was lank, their rumps were flabby, and it seemed that the women all had mustaches and the men were all bald.

As she started to fall asleep, she considered taking the next day off from the office, thought that she would call Ian and tell him the truth, tell him she was exhausted.

"Did you sleep in your panties, Zooey?" the Joyboy crooned, after awakening her at 5:30 in the morning. He chuckled his little high-pitched laugh.

Zoe hung up, happy that at least he would not call back right away—he never did. She decided that she would have to get an answering machine, after all. Changing her number had not worked. The jerk could not even pronounce her name correctly, but had somehow managed to obtain her new telephone number.

She reached for the bottle of eyedrops she always kept on the table by the bed and squeezed a drop into each eye, noticing, as she noticed each morning, that when she blinked the drops into her eyes, there was a weird whirring noise in each corresponding ear.

There was nothing to do but to go to the office early. The Joyboy had ruined any chance of sleeping late. She was grateful that her newspaper carrier always came early—the paper was usually on the porch before six. She ate grapefruit and drank coffee with her back turned to the kitchen window so that she did not have to see the couple in the house behind her drinking coffee and reading newspapers in the glare of their kitchen.

"BIZARRE BRIDGE SUICIDE TRY THWARTED" claimed a news item on the second page of the paper. Her gaze landed at once upon the item — what could have been so bizarre about it? she thought. She read that "a twenty-five-year-old man was spotted hanging from a girder by one hand and was saved by a bridge painter. The man told his rescuer that he wanted to kill himself but was afraid the fall from the bridge would be painful. He had taken a large amount of drugs and stuffed his nose with a deodorizer and was waiting for the drugs to take effect before he let go of the girder."

She could not imagine what the "deodorizer" could have been, or what it was meant to do. She had a strong impulse to telephone the county hospital and ask to speak to the young man, to ask him what it had felt like hanging over the water stoned on drugs, and if the stuff up his nose had been to keep him from smelling something. Christ, I'm as bad as the Joyboy, she thought, throwing the newspaper into the garbage pail and deciding that she would not laugh with Ian at the office about the item.

She sprayed the kitchen for ants before she left for work, wondering if the queen would be among those gassed.

No seats remained unoccupied by the time the subway train arrived at Zoe's regular departure point. She was surprised at first, but then realized it was because she usually went into the office just after the rush hour and that she was particularly early today because of the Joyboy. She stood inside the train, leaning against the back doors in spite of the sign that warned, "DANGER — do not lean against doors." She stared at the opposite pair of doors as they opened at each stop. At the city center stop, there was a handicapped man — spastic she guessed — leaning asymmetrically on two gleaming metal poles that supported his weight over turned-in knees. Her mind barely registered his presence; he was one of the mob of faces outside the train when the doors opened with their belching mechanical whir. The rest of the herd entered the car in one swift movement, briefcases swinging briskly, aerobic shoes gleaming, eyes foraging for empty seats. She saw the man thrust one of his chrome canes forward and lurch toward the doorway, and she glanced at him briefly with a momentary burst of pity. Then she saw the weight-bearing cane plunge into the narrow slot between the subway platform and the train, saw the unfortunate man's head sailing toward the ground. She threw her arms out in the man's direction, but the rest of her body remained immobile. A thin croak came from her throat as she saw his head plummet toward the concrete floor of the platform. The commuters on the platform were quicker than Zoe — they stretched their arms out to catch him before he hit the ground, but he zig-zagged crazily and missed their net. He crashed to the ground with the sound of clanging metal. The rescuers picked him up before he could lie there for more than a second; he seemed entirely unhurt. They had picked up the man quickly and silently, exchanging looks, and now were saying, "It's OK, it's all right," and leading the man onto the car as if he were blind as well. A woman jumped up from her seat so the man could sit down, but she did so discreetly — neither looking at the man nor smiling for a thank you. The man accepted the seat, not acknowledging his fall or the help he was given, not even saying thank you, but simply accepting the help and pretending nothing had happened. He sat with dignity in his seat, Zoe observed, her heart aching at his clear blue eyes and his cruel infirmity. He is so young, she thought.

She remembered quite suddenly that the same thing had happened to her once. She, too, had fallen into the slot, but had come up blushing and bleeding and wishing she had been savagely mugged or run over rather than fall down into the crack of the subway, ripping her stocking and skinning her knee. She had forgotten all about it until now. It had happened more than five years before, when she was still trapped in numb grief and despair after Dan walked out on her. She had been standing at the platform on her way to the office, clutching the *Wall Street Journal* and pretending to be reading, pretending she was still a person, a person with worldly concerns and a life. She was thinking of nothing in the world except that her back itched beneath the wool dress she wore and that it was going to be terrible having no one to scratch her back for her anymore when it broke out in wool rash, no one to scrub it in the tub with a brush when she had acne from her period. She had stepped forward into the train mechanically, just because everyone else had, and her heel had dropped efficiently down into the slot like a dime into a vending machine, and her leg followed it, all the way to the thigh. Her head was at the level of everyone else's feet for the second or two it took for a man in a dark suit to jump from his seat and pull Zoe up. Even at her moment of shame, when the man in the nice suit pulled her to her feet and said, "You're bleeding!" she realized what a neat little scene it was. She saw it as a black-and-white photograph: Photo of Woman, Chin on Ground.

Now, she tried to catch the crippled man's eye, wanted badly to say, "It happened to me, too!" but he was too smart to look into her face. He was having none of it.

Standing with her key in the office door, Zoe could hear the telephone ringing inside. She cursed when the key stuck for a second. She was irritable from lack of sleep and annoyed that Ian was not yet there, though she knew it was not eight o'clock. She picked up the phone. "Diamond Graphics."

"Zoe, it's Liz," her sister announced. "I couldn't get you at home. You'll never guess what."

"I give up," Zoe said. "What?" She could not help thinking that— knowing Liz, someone had cancer. Talking about cancer or other medical disasters brought out a zest in Liz.

"It's about Dan," Liz said, voice thrilled.

"Dan?" Zoe did not understand.

"Daniel Diamond, your former spouse?" Liz said, laughing, though not really maliciously. "Mother heard from someone who lives near Dan and his wife . . . Dan left his wife, just the way he left you! He simply came out with his suitcase and said 'sayonara bambino' or something like that." Liz paused dramatically. "What do you *think*?"

"Patsy telephoned you and told you that Dan left Cindy?" Zoe asked. She felt she was garbling the information Liz was trying to give her, scrambling it in her ears so it was unable to reach her brain.

"Yes, she asked me if I thought she should tell you, and I told her *I'd* do it," her sister said. "And you really ought to stop calling Mother 'Patsy.' Aren't you getting a little old for childish rebellion?"

"What about the kid?" Zoe asked, remembering the son Cindy delivered four years before.

"Well, Mother's friend said that Dan gave her the kid, the car, the house and the cat — that he cleaned out the bank account and said he was moving back east. So, the son is staying with Cindy, I guess."

Zoe felt a gagging sensation, was afraid she would make a retching noise over the telephone into Liz's ear. Dan had left the baby boy, just as he had left her. She was nearly able to feel a mean joy about his leaving Cindy, but all she could think of was the little boy she had never seen. Though they did not share the same blood, they shared the same last name, and now the same fate. An abandoned child, thought Zoe, oh god, oh god. She felt a violent electricity for a few seconds, thought she might be having a brain seizure — she had read about them. She heard herself say, "The boy . . . I wish I could adopt him."

"Zoe! You have always had the sickest sense of humor. Blacker than black!" trilled Liz. "Call me later when you feel like talking about it . . . I have to take Justin to gymnastics class."

Zoe stood near the phone, frowning. The child's name — it was Andy, wasn't it? Andy Diamond, an abandoned child, son of her former husband. Zoe knew she would never have a child, now. She was past thirty-five and was not even remotely involved with a man. She imagined herself as a single parent: Zoe Diamond, upwardly mobile graphic designer in her late thirties, adoptive mother of young Andrew Diamond — a child prodigy — the piano, perhaps. She would enroll the boy in the Montessori near her office, would buy him tons of gifts from Schwarz's at Christmas. During the holidays, she would no longer have to choose between sitting quietly at Liz's house, watching Liz's children rip their way through Christmas, or spending

Christmas Day with her mother and stepfather in their condominium overlooking a golf course. She would give him everything, a puppy! Everyone who knew her would be surprised that she had been able to commit herself to someone and that it was working out this time. She would have a family.

The "seizure" was over as quickly as it had begun, and the truth was self-evident. The truth: She could not stand children; she and Dan had planned not to have any. In fact, her sister's children irritated her intensely, and she often glared at unruly moppets she noticed running around in the supermarket. The fact was, she reminded herself, that little orphan Andy had a mother — he had Dan's wife, Cindy. It was a father the kid needed, not a new mother.

Before she could remove her coat and plug in the office coffee pot, the phone rang again.

"Diamond Graphics," she snapped, hating the telephone, hating everything.

"What's going on?" she heard Ian ask, his voice hostile. "Why are you in the office?"

"Obscene phone call," she said. "You know I usually come in late on Thursdays, but I've been on the damned phone since three o'clock in the morning." What did Ian care if she were in the office early?

"Zoe, have you forgotten the Staff of Life?" Ian sounded outraged. The Staff of Life was the chain of bakeries for which she and Ian had designed exterior signs and interior neon wall pieces. They had done three small bakeries and were courting the client for a new, larger bakery-café in Carmel.

"I guess I have forgotten, Ian. What about the Staff of Life?"

"Carmel! That's all. I am right now standing in a telephone booth on the corner near your house. You asked me to pick you up at eight o'clock so we could meet the Fiedlers in Carmel and visit the job site. This is Thursday, the eighth, how could you forget?"

"God, I'm sorry," she said. "What a jerk I am." She paused, then told him, "You don't really need me. Go to Carmel and tell them I got run over by a car or subpoenaed or something, and ask them if we can take them out to dinner in the City next week. It will work out."

Ian was annoyed, she knew. He was silent for a few seconds before he said that, OK, he would take care of the Fiedlers and the two of them would talk tonight on the phone.

She did not care about the Staff of Life, did not care if she and Ian went bankrupt. She thought that perhaps if she took a Tranxene and lay down on the sofa for an hour, she might be able to rest. She knew that if she were rested, not feeling so raggy and shaky, she would care about getting some work done, being productive. She would wake up with a better outlook, stop obsessing about fallen cripples and former husbands. She would feel energetic about the Staff of Life contract. She took the tablets from her handbag, removed her coat and sunglasses, and shut the blinds more tightly.

She considered telephoning her mother before she unplugged the telephone, checking to see what she might know about Dan. She did not, though; it had been only a few days since their last conversation. She had wanted to ask her mother before they hung up, "Do you love me? Mother, Patsy, my mommy, do you love your little girl?" Instead, she had said, "Say hi to Grandma." She had thought of the way she used to follow Dan around the house when they were married, asking him, "Do you love me?" — begging, no prouder than a street person asking for spare coins.

Instead of going to the water cooler with the Tranxene, Zoe walked to Ian's desk and pulled out the bottle of brandy he kept there for what the two of them termed "special occasions." She poured Ian's coffee cup half full of brandy, not bothering to rinse it out first, so that grounds and coffee sediment remained in the cup. The amount she swallowed was substantial and she flushed and felt a fast hot rush to the brain.

The cool leather of the sofa chilled her cheek when she lay down, but her chest and throat were hot from the brandy. As she closed her eyes, she suddenly remembered that she and Dan had read the Bible on their honeymoon — it had begun as a joke. They had found the

Gideon in the nightstand in their hotel room, had begun thumbing through it after drinking two bottles of champagne — feeling slightly decadent about reading the Bible in bed together, drunk and with no clothes on. Zoe had begun reading aloud from Song of Solomon, which proved erotic to them both. She had read the entire chapter aloud to Dan. Dan had said, "Darling, darling," with tears in his eyes and they had made love over and over again, knocking the Bible off the bed and to the floor.

She was stunned to awaken and see that it was nearly noon. She had been drooling onto the sofa in her sleep and sat up full of disgust for herself. A slobbering bum, passed out in her office all day while her partner did all the work. She plugged in the telephone and called the service; there had been only two calls, neither of them important.

This day was not supposed to happen, she told herself. I am going to write it off, blank it out. It is not here. I will just start over tomorrow. She called for a taxi, not feeling like taking the subway home. Her breath was sour, her mascara was smudged and there was a deep red line on her cheek from the seam in the sofa cushion. She would have the cab stop at the liquor store, and she would run in and buy some brandy and then get her shoes from the repair shop and go home. She would pay bills, or reconcile the bank statement, or she would drink all the brandy and sleep until Ian telephoned about Carmel in the evening.

She thanked god that the cabby was not a talker and was grateful that he did not say, "The meter will be running," or something equally crude before she ran into the liquor store and the shoe repair shop.

"Sole City" was the name of the shop where she had left her patent leather pumps for heel lifts. The man who owned the shop had dimmed the lights and was hanging a sign in the window that said, "Sorry You Missed Us — Back At," with a smiling cardboard clock next to it. The hands had been turned to one o'clock. She rapped quickly on the window, and the man, recognizing her, walked to the door and invited her into the semi-dark room, saying he had been on his way out to lunch.

The cobbler was a giant, standing about six feet seven inches, with huge hands, huge ears, and a very large head. Zoe had been a bit afraid of the man the first time she took her shoes there for repairs; the shop was barely larger than a closet and he dwarfed everything in the room. He had said, "May I help you?" in a deep bass voice, unsmiling, and she had felt unsettled, had a sudden irrational fear that the man might grab her and begin strangling her with his massive hands. In fact, the cobbler had been kind, wishing her a pleasant day, though his face remained mournful. She could not imagine that this dour person had named the shop "Sole City," and indeed when she inquired about the name, he said it "came with the stop" when he bought it.

As the man rummaged now in the cubbyholes at the rear of the small, darkened room, Zoe felt her initial fear of the cobbler returning, wished she had not knocked on the window and made him open up for her. She hoped the cab driver had watched her enter Sole City after she left the liquor store; she had not told him she was going to the shoe repair place. I'm nuts, she told herself, as the cobbler searched for her pumps. He is a nice man, I have a twisted mind. Her reticence about the man and the shop was no different from the fear she sometimes felt when she entered the women's room in her office complex. Every time she entered the empty restroom, she caught her breath and looked under the stalls for men's shoes—half expecting someone tough and ugly to jump from beside the toilet where he had been hiding and to punch her and rip off her skirt and tights.

The shoe man stared at Zoe, fixing his somber black eyes upon her Eisenhower jacket. She had pinned some of her father's campaign medals on the bodice, a current fashion trend. This started the man talking.

"I was in Europe during the war," he volunteered.

"Yes?" she said, smiling at him.

He pronounced each word slowly and distinctly, his voice loud but quavering. "I had it all, then," he told her. "I had the world by the *tail*."

She did not have the proper response, could not think of a suitable remark, mumbled, "I have a taxi waiting," and gestured toward the door.

She was horrified that the cobbler had preferred the war to his present circumstances. Clearly he felt himself to be rotting away in the tiny room full of smelly leather and he hated repairing the crummy footwear he was paid to salvage. She nearly ran from the shop.

Zoe overtipped the cab driver, embarrassed about the liquor store.

It was fitting, she knew, that the telephone was ringing as she entered the apartment. She could smell ant spray in the kitchen as she answered the phone.

"Tell me what turns you on, Zooey," the Joyboy demanded. He had not even said hello.

"Roses and saxophones, actually," she said.

"What?" He seemed caught off guard. It had been months since she had done anything but hang up on him.

"Roses," she said again. "And saxophones. They're both very sexy. Together, they're deadly."

"Would you like me to . . . ?"

Her timing, at least, was still there. She knew to hang up before he went any further.

Zoe poured some brandy into a coffee mug. She took the brandy into the study and pulled the Bible from a bookshelf, reading as she drank the first warm swigs: "Thy stature is like to a palm tree, and thy breasts to clusters of grapes. I will go up the palm tree, I will take hold of the boughs thereof: now also thy breasts shall be as clusters of the vine, and the smell of thy nose like apples."

lying in bed

I am naked when I wake up, which is unusual for me, because generally I sleep in a T-shirt, a men's extra-large white cotton T-shirt that hangs to my knees when I stand up. Except when I sleep with a man of course, and then I wear nothing. I have been back in the T-shirt for seven weeks, since the last time I slept with Roger — the very last time, as it turns out.

I keep looking down at my body, at the morning sunlight on my naked body where I have pulled back the covers and sheets. I keep touching my breasts, or my hand drifts down further to caress myself. I am beginning to sound like a sex magazine with "letters from readers" that say things like, "My beautiful pink nipples stood up and begged; my golden bush glinted in the sun." Still, I am sort of turning myself on.

Last night I was too tipsy when I went to bed to bother finding my T-shirt or washing off my makeup. I threw my clothes onto the floor and crawled into bed naked. Now there is lipstick and mascara all over the pillowcase and black mascara never, ever washes out.

Normally, I do not notice my body in bed. Because either I have on the T-shirt or I am — was — with Roger. It was his body I was conscious of when I woke up; the warm, lush, firm miracle of Roger's body.

I have nice breasts, though, I have to admit. The rest of me is no longer such hot material, but my breasts are actually still pretty. I wish someone else were lusting after me. Let's face it, I miss Roger and I am beginning to feel very hard-up. Oh god, I'm going to throw up.

I run to the bathroom, holding it back, and lean over the toilet just in time. I vomit, retch a few times, then open my eyes, sweating, to see the toilet bowl full of a violently red mess. Christ, I'm throwing up blood.

But I remember the Bacardi cocktails. Caitlin and I were pretty far gone last night by the time we began commanding the bartender, "Make us something pink! Anything, as long as it's pink."

I crawl back into bed, smelling bleach in my bedsheets. Only yesterday I finished purging the house of Roger's presence. I threw away his toothbrush, the ashtray he always used when he smoked — even the extra robe I kept in my closet, because he always wore it when he spent the night. I suppose I should have saved the robe for my next lover, but I'll probably never have one, and besides, I do not want to think of Roger for any reason. I stripped the bed yesterday, removed the mattress pad, ran it through the washer and drier and used plenty of Clorox. Now it is a pure, chaste white again. Not a trace of Roger's yellowish semen left in my bed. No sign, either, of the clear, warm liquid that gushed from me when Roger and I made love. God, it was embarrassing the first time it happened, but Roger liked it. He used to whisper things in my ear at those times, saying, "Oh, baby, I'm in a tropical rain forest," or "Sure, let's go for a warm swim together," and I would have laughed out loud if I hadn't been going crazy at the time. Afterward, he would point to the soaked sheets and say, "Really, Zoe, we ought to take you on tour," and then I would laugh.

Well, the sheets are plenty dry now. At least mine are.

No hearts of gold, no nerves of steel, that's what the song says, and it has been running through my head for days, over and over again. I was chanting it last night after the pink drinks — I like to say it backward, too — no nerves of gold, no hearts of steel — and Caitlin finally told me I was too drunk and that we had better call a taxi.

This is going to be one of the days when I never get out of bed. It used to happen about once a year, maybe during my annual Christmas neurosis, but this will be the second time in seven weeks that I have spent an entire Sunday in bed.

Tools of the trade. Those are the things I need to gather about me in order to have a decent day alone in bed. I will get the tools of the trade right now so that I do not even have to move again unless I have to go to the bathroom, or—god forbid—throw up again. The telephone, the decanter of ruby port, the morning newspaper, a book, and some Motrin for my hangover. Everything I need. Except. But don't even think about that. Block it out *right* now! Or you will start obsessing over the R word.

The telephone rings just as I pick it up from the desk. Startled, I shriek, then answer calmly, "Yes?"

"*Yes?* Get off it, Zoe," Caitlin says.

"I threw up red stuff . . . the pink drinks," I tell her.

"Oh, sorry, you poor kid. I have a cruel headache myself."

"What's up, Cait?"

"I wondered if you're up to a little hair of the dog," she says. "Want to go for Bloody Marys and brunch?"

"Just what I need, more red."

"Are you really sick?"

"No," I admit. "I felt fine once I barfed. It's just that I'm sort of crazy today. I don't want to get out of bed."

"Then you *should*," she says. "Why are you *wallowing*? What's all this junk about 'nerves of steel?' Have you thought of going back to Dr. Franklin for crisis intervention?"

"What's the crisis?" I demand.

"You're being belligerent," Caitlin says.

A pal always knows. I just sit here, looking away from the telephone receiver.

"Zoe, it's not terribly normal to spend every weekend lying in bed drinking port. All this sulking and acting-out over Roger is certainly a waste. Buck up kiddo. Come to life.

"I've had my period *three* times since I've made love," I whine. "Three times! This is a first."

"Then you're lucky," she says. "I've gone for months and months without a lover in my life and it didn't kill me off. Besides, you get your period about every week and a half. It's stress related."

"I know," I say. But I do not know. "I'll snap out of it. This is my last day in bed." I am lying. I am a bigger liar than anyone in the world, even R. "Just let me have one last day in bed," I beg, wanting her to mother me.

"Okay, Zoe, have it your way," she says. "Be a good girl and drink up all your port and read until you pass out, and don't forget to go into the office in the morning or Ian will find a new partner."

"No, he likes the name 'Diamond Graphics'; he always tells me so. Can you imagine 'Berger Graphics'?"

"He'll strike your name and call the business after his new partner — one of his little boyfriends," Caitlin says.

"He'll always love me best," I insist.

"He just wants to sleep with his mother," she says. "If you slept with him or if you were his own age, you'd bore him."

"Yes." I laugh. "R always said Ian wanted to kill me and then fuck my body."

"Well, that's unkind," Caitlin says. "Besides, Ian is a good partner, right? You couldn't really do without him."

"Nope. He's a good partner and he's actually a better graphic artist than I am, if you want to know the truth."

"We'll have lunch this week," she says. "Don't cry all day, for godsake."

I say that I will not, another lie, and then I say goodbye.

My quilt is blue. I need serene colors on my bed or I have insomnia. Once I had red sheets and they gave me headaches. The blue is soothing, but I am blue, too. I am very blue, so I pour myself a nice glass of ruby port, knowing that when I finish it I will be loose enough for a crying jag. I often tell people at parties that I am going to buy a Jaguar and get personalized license plates that say "CRYING," but the truth is I am not. I am not even going to buy an old dirtbag Toyota. I will continue to drive my beat-up station wagon, or I will drive Ian's Audi when I have to meet with a client.

The blue of the quilt blurs as the first tears of self-pity begin to fill my eyes. I remember that I read an item in a Sunday supplement that said blue is the only color birds cannot see. How strange the sky must be for them.

"I am very blue," I say aloud.

I pick up the newspaper, and on the front page, right next to a story about terrorist bombings is a story headed "MEN'S BODY ODOR CAN HELP WOMEN." Amen, I think. The news report says that scientists have established that the aromatic chemical compounds called "pheromones," which the body excretes primarily as a sexual attractant, can actually affect the sexual physiology of others. The study found that "women who have sex with men at least once a week are more likely to have normal-length menstrual cycles." I'll have to tell that to Caitlin. The article says that the male chemicals are secreted from the armpits, around the nipples, and in the genital region.

I refill my glass with port. Oh, R, the way you smelled. Yes, I remember the smell near your nipples—you nearly had to pry me off your chest in the morning.

Aromatic chemicals near your genitals? Yes. And I was afraid of you there at first. I looked at you and thought, This is overkill, could be unwieldy. It was overkill, all right. When we made love, I felt as if I had been turned inside out like a stocking.

You lied, though, R, just like everyone else. For godsake, even Richard Pryor turned out to be a big liar. I had always admired him for being so honest in his comedy routines. Once he even went on television and told the world he grew up in a brothel. But after that he told Barbara Walters during an interview that he had not been freebasing when he caught fire, that there had been an "accident" with rum and matches. This is what good liars do to you: They throw you off track by feeding you a few really honest secrets, then they lie to you, their faces heartbreaking masks.

The telephone rings again. It is Ian. "Zoe," my business partner says, "I hate to bug you on a Sunday—I know you're always in the middle of something."

Yes, I think. I am in the middle of a blue quilt.

"No, it's fine, Ian. What's going on?"

"I need to take tomorrow off," he says. "My parents are coming up from Santa Barbara this afternoon and will be here a couple of days. I need to take them out, be nice to them. Can you get into the office a few minutes early tomorrow and meet with Cliff Hinckley at eight?"

"Eight?" I croak.

"He has to be at the airport by 9:30. I told him we could show him the work we've done since last time he came in. Do you mind terribly?"

"No, Ian, it's fine."

"What are you doing?" he wants to know.

"I'm lying in bed."

"This late? Roger-the-rod must have reentered the scene," he says. His tone is joking, but I feel the meanness.

"Roger's gone, Ian," I say. "I'm alone and depressed."

"*Alone* in bed? Get up then!" He is so chipper that I want to slam the phone down in his ear. "What could be worse than being in bed alone on a sunny Sunday?" he says.

"Being in bed with a rat would be worse," I reply.

"I thought Roger *was* a rat," he says.

"I meant a real one, a rodent." There is a silence and I realize that Ian is beginning to wonder if I need to go back onto my medication. "A rat got into bed with my friends Ruby and John when they were living in Hawaii," I tell him.

"No!" He says. "Really?"

"At first Ruby thought it was John moving next to her, but it wasn't. There was a huge rat right in the covers with them, and when she woke John up, he wouldn't believe her."

"I'm not sure I do, either," Ian says.

"Men never believe women," I say, too shrilly. "Ruby had to cry and beg before John would get up and turn on the light, and then they saw a great big rat dive off the bed and go under some furniture. John finally shot the thing with a pellet gun, or some kind of a gun—I forget."

"What was he doing with a gun?" Ian asks, sounding prim.

"Well, they were marijuana farmers," I say.

"I never get used to your sordid past, Zoe. No one would believe it all, to know you now. You have a million of these stories and I know they're all true. Just be careful who you tell them to."

It is my turn to feel mean. I feel like saying, "Yeah, Ian, and don't tell your parents about all the hours you've logged in the baths," but I say nothing.

After Ian hangs up, I empty my glass of port in one gulp, though it gags me a bit, and I refill the glass from the decanter. The port makes me feel flushed, and I say, "I am red and blue," and dial Roger's number. I listen to the phone ring for a long time, imagining his empty flat, wondering if his telephone is really ringing if there is no one there to hear it.

I visualize Roger's unmade bed—doubtless the sheets are beautifully stained. I see the dishes stacked up in the kitchen, and I know that he will be out of paper towels, because he uses them as plates when all the dishes are dirty. I was never in love with a slob before, but the good thing about his sloppiness was that it was an excuse for us not living together. "God, we could *never* live together," I often said, mostly because he had long ago ceased asking me to move in with him.

It infuriates me that a man, and a slob at that, can do this to me. Why am I paralyzed because Roger left me? What am I, some kind of a wallflower?

Yes. I am the girl who was not asked to the senior prom.

"Watch Zoe Banks show up in a see-through dress," they all said at the prom. "She'll get here about midnight with a playboy on one arm and two fairies on the other." I spent prom night watching a basketball game on television with my family, having told my parents I was not going because it was too juvenile.

Roger, you bastard. I cannot even go to a movie, because when couples kiss on the screen, I burst into tears. Ever try to find a film with no kissing in it? Christ, they even kiss in the Disney movies, now. You can see their animated tongues moving, if you look closely.

I cannot read magazines, either, because there are always breasts in magazines. Bare breasts are stylish in the ads. I see them and imagine the breasts Roger is fondling and kissing. I would gladly murder both of them, hack them to death.

The phone again. This time the ringing does not even startle me. The port has begun to numb me, just as I planned.

"Zoe?" It is Roger. He sounds like the same old charlatan. He sounds like he wants to come back. I am amazed to hear what sounds like parrots squawking in the background.

I think I will tell him I have been tattooed, that my body is now covered with snakes. No—I will tell him I am marrying a man with skin like coffee, a client from Jamaica. I will tell him that in the last seven weeks, I have learned the meaning of the word love.

"Who would have guessed," I will say, "that old Reverend Roy was right when he said on television that prayer can make you rich? I'm richer than the devil now."

faithful

Every time Zoe sneezes, she expects rose petals to fly from her nose. She saw this once, as a child. A young cousin had torn up a rose and stuffed the petals up her nose, then begun a sneezing fit. With each explosion from the little girl's nose, red petals spewed into the air like blood and then drifted beautifully to the ground.

"Bless you," Roger says, unbuttoning the back of her blouse.

"Bless you too," she says, feeling his beard and lips brush the skin on her back. Before he can go for the zipper on her skirt, she asks, "Was I wearing one girdle or two before we broke up?"

"Oh, Zoe," he says gravely, shaking his head and looking pained. "You wear two now?"

"Yes," she confesses. "I still wear the stretchy black lace one I had before, but now I wear a more powerful one underneath it."

"Why wear the black one if the other one is so 'powerful'?" Roger says.

"The powerful one's ugly — I'm trying to cover it up."

Roger sighs as he unzips her.

She had been slim before the breakup, then lost five pounds while she was not seeing Roger. But she still felt bulky, matronly — hated seeing the soft swell of her abdomen when she undressed. She decided on the Playtex "18-Hour Girdle," size "Small," beige elastic.

Roger has her skirt off in no time and makes short work of the two panty-girdles and the pair of tights. He slides his hands under the bikini underpants before pulling them down, touches her where it counts.

"Twenty layers to get to you," he complains, but there is humor in his voice. His expression is sultry as he stares at her pelvis. He tells her that her pubic hair is beautifully, artistically placed — "perfect." She wonders, compared to whose? and thinks about condoms.

She sees the newspaper carrier walking away from her house after throwing the morning paper onto the porch. It is cold and still semi-dark and he has his head bowed against the wind. He is wearing a hooded gray sweatshirt to protect himself from the cold during his deliveries. He is an acned boy of about sixteen who is never late. It suddenly breaks her heart this child must get out of bed every day before dawn and go out into the frigid mornings to earn a few dollars.

I'm getting my period early, she surmises as the tears come to her eyes. She knows the paper boy is not really piteous enough to cry over, so the tears must be caused by hormones.

The gloom continues. At the subway station the escalator is broken and the staircase is drenched with what looks like blood. She steps delicately over the pools of deep, fresh red, pretending not to notice them. She wonders where the bleeder has gone — the spill looks recent, but there is no sign of a fight or a stricken body. She recalls the time in the same subway station when she saw a black man lying on the stairs bleeding from the forehead. She had been forced to step over him, numb except for the thought that he looked like a chocolate cherry that had been bitten into and tossed down.

One of her neighbors, a man who always smiles at her, is waiting for the train. "Hi, Zooey," he says, grinning, saying her name wrong, but in the nicest way. "How goes it today?"

"I don't know," she says, "I woke up sad. And now this blood on the stairs." She gestures toward the crimson pools.

He laughs as if he will die and slaps her on the arm. "That's not blood, it's soda," he tells her. She notices he is carrying the special edition of the morning newspaper, which features a full-page color photo of the pope and details of his impending U.S. tour. He points to the red puddles on the stairs and says, "Look! It's cherry soda or somethin'."

She says that, yes, she guesses it is cherry soda and that maybe her dark glasses were responsible for the mistake, but she moves away from him as quickly as possible, thinking, why does he refuse to see it's blood?

Once on the train, she is seized by panic. She has the fear: What if it *is* cherry soda and I am seeing blood? She considers getting off the train and riding back one station to double-check her perception, but she does not. Her breasts sting; she knows it is her period after all.

Ian is meeting with a client and Zoe is alone in their office, drinking strong coffee and working on the new logo for Beefy Burger. She finds herself repeatedly sketching hamburgers with human faces and extremities, fat and mean looking with sinister smiles. She begins to feel hungry as she works on the sketches. Her stomach growls at the thought of a burger.

She decides to take a break and go over to the greasy spoon down the block for a burger on a hard roll with bleu cheese, rare.

Before she puts her coat on, she walks over to the supply room in the back of the office and peers in. She and Ian have found mouse droppings in their desk drawers and near the hot plate in the supply room. She is terrified of rodents and had wanted to call an exterminator immediately, but Ian laughed at her and told her he would put out a couple of traps. Even the sight of the empty trap placed discreetly between two boxes of computer paper in the supply room makes her feel spooked and the hair stands up on her arms. She cannot decide which is worse: the rodents still being loose in the office, or the thought of actually seeing a smashed one in the trap.

"Daddy-Joe's" is half-empty, as it always is. The front door is open wide and a cold breeze fills the burger joint. The television behind the counter is on and she takes a table as far from it as possible so that she does not have to see or hear the game show that is on. The pink plastic carnations in the bud vase on her table are dusty, and the green fronds of the fake ferns hanging from the ceiling are broken off in places, leaving brittle stubs. There is no burger in the city that can rival "Daddy-Joe's Blue Burger," however.

"A Blue Burger, very rare and a glass of white wine," Zoe tells the young waitress.

"I know," the waitress says, smiling. "I already wrote it down," she tells her, bustling off, pleased with herself. "You're a regular," she calls over her shoulder.

No, I'm not! Zoe wants to protest, shocked, and has to cough to keep from saying something unkind. She does not want to be considered a "regular" in a depressing greasy spoon.

From the window near her table, she can see a construction project she has been watching for months. A huge row of buildings had been demolished in one morning, leaving dust and debris and rodents. The new building, a high-rise, began going up immediately. She can see a muscular young man welding, and her eyes are riveted to him. He is holding the acetylene torch high above his head and bright green stars fly from it like Fourth of July sparklers. Aside from his hard hat and some long leather gloves, he is wearing only tight jeans and a tank top, and she can see the deep black of his underarm hair burgeoning from beneath the upraised arm. She immediately thinks of Roger and feels the same rush of blood that has always overwhelmed her at the thought of him.

Her passion for Roger is constant, but her trust of him comes and goes. "I'm sick to death of having to take you on sheer faith!" she screamed at him the last time they broke up. It is always his "grandmother's" lipstick that rolls out from under the front seat of his car. If she sees him having coffee in a café with a woman at eight o'clock in the morning, he says it is a coworker he ran into on the way to work. "How dare you question my integrity!" he has shouted, acting as if it is she who is at fault.

"The last two years I was married," she hears the woman at the table behind her say to her friend, "my husband wouldn't even have sex with me on my birthday. The least I expected, as a courtesy for goodness sake, was to get laid on my birthday."

The friend answers, "When I was married, it was sort of understood that as a gift, I wouldn't have to on my birthday."

Both women laugh, but Zoe does not even smile. She is reminded of her marriage to Jack — "that fairy" as her father had always referred to her husband behind her back. Yet it had been Jack who wanted to make love all the time. "That fairy" had been an ardent lover, but Zoe had felt like vomiting every time he touched her. She had often pretended to have a vaginal infection for months at a time to avoid contact with him.

She signals the waitress she would like the burger to go, instead, and takes the burger and an individual-sized bottle of chablis back to the office with her.

When she sits down to her desk, she hears it: The trap has gone off. She freezes, too nauseated to eat, and wonders if the trap now holds a huge mean rat by the tail, or perhaps a squashed field mouse. Her heart races and she sits perfectly still in her swivel chair. She is filled with revulsion and cannot decide whether to go in and look at the trap or not. To her horror, she hears the trapped rodent squeak, twice, and hears the trap rattling as the creature thrashes. She sits motionless until the sounds of struggle cease, then tiptoes toward the supply room to investigate. The mouse turns its tiny gray head toward her, lifting its neck from the small plank to look her full in the face. She runs out of the office to the parking lot, though she has not brought her car that day. Her only thought is, What if it is a female? The resigned gentility of the manner in which the mouse had waited for its death, and the delicate way it had raised its head to look at her, made her gruesomely think of the old song about a woman dying: Miss Otis regrets, she's unable to lunch today.

She awakens at three in the morning with a persistent grinding in her abdomen and gets up to go to the bathroom. In the dark of the hallway, she feels a sudden splash onto her bare insteps and hears a rapid dripping on the oakstrip flooring. Oh, god, I'm wetting my pants, she thinks — a thought made worse by the knowledge that she is naked. She switches on the bathroom light and sees that her feet are covered in red rivulets and that there are curvy pink lines wiggling their way down the insides of her legs. She grabs some toilet paper and a damp sponge and runs back to the hall, where there is a pool of blood and a trail of red droplets. She sponges it from the floor, holding toilet paper between her legs, thinking, I am not pregnant, for approximately the two hundred fortieth time. The blood looks curiously like cherry soda, and she begins laughing aloud in a high-pitched bark until she hears Roger call out, "What's wrong?" from the bedroom.

"Nothing," she says. "Just a menstrual accident, go back to sleep." She wonders how he heard her. He has begun wearing earplugs to bed since they resumed seeing each other after the last round of suspicion and anger. He says he cannot sleep without the plugs in his ears because she gets up so many times during the night.

"If it's not you wandering the house all night, clomping around," Roger complains, "it's that dog of yours crying outside the bedroom door."

Usually at some point after they make love, while they are still talking and hugging before they fall asleep, he sneaks the plugs discreetly into his ears. She will be talking or laughing at those times, head on the fragrant curls of his chest, and sometimes he will not respond to what she has said. She will reach up gently then and touch his ear, finding that it is plugged and that he has not been listening to her at all.

"PAPAL ALTAR COLLAPSES IN HIGH WINDS," she reads in the newspaper the morning of her appointment with Dr. Dennis. The pope's U.S. tour is going badly, it seems. It rained in Miami and the Mass there had to be halted. Now, the two 150-foot tapestry-covered decorative towers for the papal Mass in Texas have been blown down before the pope's arrival.

Zoe snickers meanly and wonders if the pope mobile will crack up next. She does not wish the man to be hurt, certainly, but she immensely enjoys every loss of dignity for the king of a church that wants women pregnant all over the world. She cannot comprehend why "The Holy Father" is not laughed at when he rides about in his pope mobile saying things such as, "John Paul II, he loves you, too," with his Bela Lugosi Dracula accent.

Dr. Dennis is going to give her a shot in the arm. The injection will interrupt and eventually terminate her menstrual cycle. He has explained to her on the telephone that this will end the hemorrhaging and the erratic mood swings she has been going through. It will also serve as a contraceptive for three full months.

"You should use your diaphragm, anyway," Dr. Dennis had cautioned. "Just in case." She knows from looking the drug up in the reference library that this is because a fetus accidentally conceived after the shot could be born horribly deformed. She had said OK to Dr. Dennis about the diaphragm with a serious tone and a heart full of irony. As if I'd *have* the kid, in any case, she thought.

Sometimes, when she is driving her car, Zoe sees couples dancing as she looks through the lighted windows of houses. She will see them through shutters, or whirling past open drapes, around and around, the kitchen lights bright behind them. She has wondered if it is voyeuristic to watch couples dancing like this, zooming by in her car and then slowing to catch them whirling and turning tenderly. Sometimes she sees it is two men, and then it is not exactly as romantic as it seemed at first, but romantic just the same. A gay couple waltzing in the dining room is much better than no couple dancing at all, as in her own flat. She knows Roger still dances—she can tell from the matchbooks she sees when he lights his cigarettes. The DV8 and the Paradise and all the hip dance spots south of Market—he goes there and dances, but she does not. She drives around alone in her car watching men with crew cuts embracing in their apartments.

She and Roger met at a dance two years ago. He had mimicked the way she danced, with a slight smirk on his face and she fell for him right then and there. He told her later he'd thought she dressed and danced like Charlie Chaplin and that he had loved her at first glimpse. They used to dance together in her living room after sharing a bottle of brandy, laughing and kissing and sometimes falling right down. Roger tells her now that he likes "earthy" women. She checks the dictionary and finds it defined as "coarse, unrefined." She knows Roger does not find her earthy . . . a Charlie Chaplin woman is not earthy.

Sometimes she dances alone, but she makes certain the shades are pulled tight and that there is no light for a backdrop.

Ian telephones from the office, saying, "We got a mouse."

"Yes," Zoe answers.

"You knew?" Ian says, outraged. "Thanks a lot for getting rid of the stiff. The office stank to high heaven when I got in this morning."

"I'm sorry," Zoe says. "I was too squeamish, and besides I started thinking what if it had babies in the nest or something and I sort of freaked."

Ian says nothing. The silence is awkward.

"I'm sorry, OK?" she says again, with a menacing tone.

Ian lets it go by, changes the subject. "The whole neighborhood is getting ready for the pope," he says. Ian lives near Mission Dolores, where the Hispanic Catholic and the gay neighborhoods overlap. "Rex and I spent all day yesterday painting and hanging a big banner that says 'The Pope Is A Schmuck', " he says.

She is surprised to find herself bristle. "I think that's rude," she says. "The pontiff is like a visiting head of state; people should behave decently."

"Oh, yeah, a visiting head of state, like the pope described that Nazi Waldheim! And what do you mean '*the pontiff*' — since when are you a Catholic, girl?"

This reminds her of a family dinner many years ago. In the kitchen, tipsy and talkative after wine, she had confessed to her mother, "I think I'm secretly religious."

Her mother had paused, then said, "Well, I suppose it's better than being secretly queer, dear."

Zoe begins discussing the Beefy Burger contract in order to avert a quarrel. She tells Ian, too, that she will call an exterminator and pay for it out of her personal funds rather than from the office account.

"I can't face any more dead things," she tells him. "There was blood coming out of her mouth as she died, Ian. She squeaked for godsake."

"You are one twisted wreckage," Ian says, laughing. "Want to go to the new Louis Malle film tonight?"

She says that yes, she will go to the film. She says that Roger has to work tonight.

She is still trembling, though they have turned the electric blanket on and Roger is holding her tightly. They have made love all night — Zoe sobbing and shaking, Roger forgetting not to shout — and the sun is coming up.

"Thank god it's Sunday," she says, teeth chattering. "It's really bad when we do this and I hear the alarm go off in the middle of things and realize I have to get up and go to the office."

She had come home from the film after midnight and had been surprised to find Roger in her bed, smoking in the dark. Her Great Dane was curled up next to him on the bed and had not even come to the door to greet Zoe.

"Hello, beautiful," he said quietly as she approached the bedroom.

She was glad to see him. He had been evasive about his plans for that night and she had not pressed him. This was only the second time he had used the key she had given him to her flat. The other time, he had let himself in on her birthday to throw glitter and confetti all over her flat and to put champagne in the refrigerator. He had never offered her a key to his house, making it understood that he thought it would annoy his housemates.

From the feel of things, Roger is ready again. She does not take the bait, says, "I think this is all that's left for us, Roger. I think at this point it's just sex."

"Just?" Roger says. He laughs lazily and lights a cigarette. "Do you know what most people would do for a chance at something like you and I have in bed together? 'Just sex,' that's rich."

"We don't share anything else, we don't do anything together anymore, we don't have anything except this." Roger's body is hot against her quaking back. "We used to both be dying to see the same films all the time, remember? And when I woke you up in the night that time and asked if you could remember which philosopher was the 'either/or guy,' you mumbled 'Kierkegaard,' kissed my neck and fell back asleep. Now you wouldn't even hear me!"

"Oh, no," he says. "This is the speech that always comes before a woman says, 'I think we should get married.'"

She feels a hot burst of rage. "I don't want to marry you. And I didn't realize you'd been proposed to so many times, poor dear."

"Well, if you don't want to marry me, why are you acting like you want to get married? Is it that maybe you want to marry someone else, that you're wasting your time with me when you could be lining up your third bridegroom?"

"It's that you don't want to marry *me*," she says, pulling the bedsheet up over her breasts. "I can't understand why if you really do love me you'd rather live with housemates and sleep here only two or three times a week. I wonder why I always miss you and you never seem to miss me, that's all."

"Then why don't you want to marry me?"

"You're too sloppy," Zoe tells him. "You really are the worst slob in the world, Roger. Why do you have to live that way?" But she is crying, letting the tears drip onto her pillowcase and make little pools, hoping he will not see them. She has not until this moment realized that she, with her tidy house and a bed filled more often by a Great Dane than a man, is desolate. Roger is happy with his messy house and his "freedom." He can dance with earthy women. She has a lover who sleeps wearing earplugs so he cannot hear her say she loves him.

Zoe changes into her robe when she gets home from the office, glad to pull off the two girdles and the stockings and the wool dress which has been making her back itch all day. She tears off the Band-Aid Dr. Dennis put on her arm the previous day after the injection. He had advised her she might become a little bloated and had cautioned her again to use her diaphragm as back-up.

"I won't be needing that, now," she told him.

He put his arm around her, sweet and effeminate as he has been for the entire fifteen years she has been his patient, saying, "Boyfriend problems?" and patting her gently on the back. "Those never last," he said. "Especially not for a pretty woman like you."

Boy are you dumb, she thought, but smiled and said nothing. She left his office excited about being free of her periods and yet feeling strangely sexless, neutered.

"Jocasta! You're too big to do that," she tells her dog as it jumps up on her and kisses her face. "Down, girl, and stay down," she warns, but bends to kiss the dog's big, smooth head.

She pours herself a brandy and decides to skip dinner and just climb straight into bed and vegetate in front of the tube until she falls asleep. She pulls the covers down and motions Jocasta to jump up and lie on what had been Roger's side of the bed. She pats Jocasta on the rump, thinking the dog is the only good thing left from her second marriage. In fact, she had been the *only* thing left from the marriage — Dan had taken all the furniture, cleaned out the bank account, and left Jocasta and a pile of bills for Zoe.

She presses the remote control button three times, but the pope is on every station. The local archbishop has wonderful black eyebrows like two caterpillars and she stops at the station that has the camera on him, knowing him to be a humane and rather liberal priest. She watches the pope being escorted into Mission Dolores, past the protesters and throngs of the pious who have stood outside all day, waiting. She imagines she spots Ian's "The Pope Is a Schmuck" banner as the cameras pan the neighborhood, but in fact there are many caustic banners, and there are groups of men dressed as nuns, chanting insults.

A little high fashion goes a long way, she thinks, as she watches the pope in his beautifully detailed white dress and cap move down the aisle of the Mission, attended by droves of starkly black-robed, scarlet-sashed priests. Before the Mass, the pope spends a great deal of time praying at the altar, the camera so close that privacy is impossible for him. In fact, though the pope's face is serious, prayerful, even tortured, the camera catches him stealing a glimpse at his wristwatch. He is a handsome man, she thinks, remembering the rumors about him as a young actor in his native country. As the singing and praying begin, Zoe is shocked to find herself moved, taken in by the pageantry and by the pope's own enigmatic personality, a scholarly man in a stunning white gown. She feels sentimental and blames it on the brandy. Those Catholics really know how to put on a show, she thinks, but she says to Jocasta, "Look, girl, it's the Holy Father; isn't he lovely?" and puts her arm around the dog's neck.

She has a horrible thought: What if he is right? What if he's right and I'm wrong? At the same instant, she remembers her friend Rusty Woods, the sculptor. One night during the seventies, he went into his bedroom, came out with a pistol, and shot the television set. The television smoked, and then Rusty put the gun away, never saying a word.

She sneezes. The dog's bristly hairs are irritating her nose. She says, "Bless me," then sneezes again and again. Her eyes are closed, but she knows without looking that with each spasm, red rose petals fill the room.

victoria

cinema verite

Bette Davis was probably responsible for my wedding gown. I insisted on a bright red dress, and my mother knew better than to try to talk me out of it. She had tried to talk me out of marrying Peter and now realized she had only firmed my resolve.

We had a small family wedding, after an eight-year engagement. Certainly there must be other eight-year engagements, but I have never known of one. The length of our prenuptial involvement was not due to one of us being in graduate school, nor to any other solid reason. We simply — that is, he simply — kept putting it off. When we finally firmed up the wedding date, we both had a shadowy awareness of the fact that any change whatever in the relationship would be a blessing.

I more or less sprinted to the altar, my father tagging behind me and my crimson gown flapping about my booted legs. Barbara Stanwyck was probably responsible for my boots.

When the reception had been in progress for a few hours and the bouquet had been caught by one of Peter's fat nieces, I took Peter home to my apartment like a newly acquired pet. The day of the wedding Peter had brought in his stereo system and his collection of memorabilia; and I had cleared off fifty percent of the bedroom bureau top for him and emptied one-third of the drawer and closet space. I felt alternately titillated by my apartment's new, masculine image and irritated at my turf being invaded. The best of the lot was his record collection, several thousand strong and beginning with Bill

Haley and the Comets. The worst was a hair ball which had been found within the innards of a slaughtered steer in the meat packing plant where one of Peter's uncles worked. It was as smooth as a crystal vase, and when one looked closely, it resembled a tightly wound ball of very silky thread. Guests often picked it up, rubbing their palms over its surface and saying, "Ooh, what's this?" Some, as I, were repelled, asking, "Really?" and putting it quickly back on the table. But most were fascinated and would closely examine the sphere. The marijuana smokers would usually take the ball into a corner, fondling it and peering closely at it for the remainder of the evening. I found myself wondering what made some persons hair ball haters and what made others interested students of hair balls. Was it a genetic trait, like the color of one's eyes?

The first few weeks were blissful for us; coziness became a state of mind. Neither of us had ever lived with anyone before, and we found it soothingly pleasing to do so now. After living alone as I had for so long, I found myself glowing with smiles when I came home in the evenings. Walking up the hill from the train station, I could see my — our — window lighted up. How wonderful to walk into a warm, bright apartment instead of a chilly, night-filled one. When I opened the door, Pat Metheny's or Darol Anger's music leapt out to greet me, and Peter called out, "Hey, Vicks," from the bedroom, where he would be working at the desk. We drank zinfandel out of the pewter goblets my coworkers had given us as a wedding present, and we ate huge red apples and sharp cheddar, also wedding gifts from friends. We felt as happy and corny as the lyrics to the old Crosby Stills and Nash albums we still listened to. "Our house . . ."

Peter was a film buff, too, and we spent hundreds of hours in lines together over the years, wanting to be among the first to see the really big ones. By an odd fluke, we missed seeing *Midnight Cowboy*, so when it came back around, we were exultant. We went to see it on a week night; it was playing at the Cine-Art for two dollars. Our life was not to be the same after the advent of Ratso.

Peter had begun smoking cigarettes three days before our wedding, and I smoldered with resentment over it. He gave no reason for the new habit and refused to give it up, though I pleaded. The apartment stank, and there were ashtrays all over the house crammed with unsightly butts. It was painfully obvious to me that this was his way of getting back at me for finally getting him to the altar. So ya' want to play rough? I thought bitterly to myself.

"God, I really related to Ratso," Peter said at breakfast the morning after *Midnight Cowboy*.

"Why? His cough remind you of your own developing smoker's hack?" I said, not looking up from the morning newspaper.

"I see myself ending up exactly like that," he said. "I've always known it." He slowly buttered the toast which he had intentionally burned black. I looked at him, trying to imagine what he was visualizing. He sat at the breakfast table, the sun making rainbows on his thick, reddish-black hair; his shoulders were broad beneath the navy velour robe. He was a tall, handsome young man, looking more like a football star than an anthropology professor. He was bright, healthy, and came from a comfortable suburban family. "Do you mean you think you're going to die young, or what?" I queried.

"I just mean I identify with him," he said casually, leafing through the sports section of the newspaper. "I can see myself in a room like that, alone like that, living on the edge . . . I am Ratso."

I got up and poured myself a fifth cup of coffee. I saw it now. My husband, the man I had elected to spend my life with, the father of my prospective children, felt a deep affinity with Rico Rizzo, a.k.a. "Ratso." Rico Rizzo: cripple, New York street person, con artist. Friendless, dying, desperate Ratso, living in an abandoned tenement building, coughing his insides out. "You are Ratso," I murmured, and buried my face in the medical advice column in the newspaper. The subject was how to rid oneself of crab lice.

When I met David, Peter and I had been married less than six months. The trouble had already begun by then, though it was Peter who thought of it as trouble, not I. I thought of it as fun. My belle-of-the-ball phase was in full flower, and I was dizzy with it. All the years I had been engaged to Peter, I had played the role of devoted fiancée. On the shelf, as it were. I had flirted with no one, for I had found early on that even a friendly smile or casual conversation had invited suitors who were not deterred when I told them I was engaged. So, I had routinely snubbed men and waited for Peter. Since our marriage, I found myself reveling in my new role as the young wife. I could flirt all evening with the most handsome men at parties we attended, and I felt free to dance groin-to-groin with numerous fellows, for I would be going home with my husband and everyone knew it. It was a heady experience to play the tease and not be expected to pay for it. Peter was grim and pained over the change in me, and after a particularly festive Valentine's Day party we attended, during which he had totally lost sight of me for three hours, he had a mournful chat with me in the morning. Shaking his head, he said, "Vicky, I could always trust you, before—I never even had to think about it. I never had to worry about anyone getting to you. Now, it's like I don't even know you."

"Don't be silly," I said. Right, Ratso, I thought.

David was a proud person; all would turn to look at him just because of the way he walked into a room. He wore an understated air of confidence and poise. One could not imagine him in an awkward situation. He was magnetic without being showy or coming on too strong. "Wait 'till you meet the new junior partner," a coworker had told me. "He's to die over."

"Another flashy lover-boy for the office? Who cares?" I said.

"We'll see," she said and smiled.

And so, I loved him at first sight, and then I hated him because he looked like a small boy when he smiled and because he seemed not one bit impressed with me. And then, we talked all afternoon at an office party held in a sunny plaza outside our building and I loved him again. I began to love him recklessly. He had thin, very red lips that were a magnet for my own full, pale lips. His beard was blonde and black and red and brown, and I knew that it would smell fresh and fragrant as wet grass when I kissed him. He had a rich, vivid-sounding laugh. I noticed when lunching with David that we were always shown to the very best table, even if neither of us had ever been in that particular restaurant before.

We began meeting every morning at the train station. I would be breathless all the way up the Peninsula, my head filled with David the way it used to be filled with Santa on Christmas Eve. I would fly from the train and there would be his ancient green Volvo, and I would jump into it, and probably the first few weeks we just smiled ourselves half to death, but after that we grabbed at each other's faces and hair, raining kisses on each other, mumbling, "Darling, Darling," like a mantra and burying our faces in each other's coats. The smell of his tweed jacket and his hair was in my mind every second we were apart.

The winos were the only ones who knew about us, and they approved wholeheartedly. David parked his car every morning on Minna Street in a park-it-yourself lot—the type with a little coin box instead of an attendant. We would talk and kiss there before walking to the office. There was a thriving skid row in the area. Commuters walking briskly from the train station routinely stepped over fallen winos and broken Thunderbird bottles, taking no apparent notice. Sometimes David and I would see large rats strolling about the parking lot. It was an odd trysting spot, but we never saw anyone we knew there. The sun shone dazzlingly off the broken glass and the chrome auto bumpers in the mornings; we felt showered by radiance. Walking down Third Street together, we must have looked as love-struck as we were, for fairly regularly a group of derelicts leaning against a building would call out to us, "That's it kids!" or raise their brown bags to us in a toast, saying, "Yeah, be in love, be in love." We would feel a thrill that our love was visible: That meant it really did exist. But before the financial district, we would touch hands and part, trying to purge all signs of passion from our countenances and look as grim as everyone else as we walked separately the last two blocks. Only the bums must know.

Casablanca was playing again on television one weekend, and Peter and I watched it together at home. We did so out of Sunday afternoon boredom and because we liked Bogie. Peter was touched by the film, and once or twice I saw his eyes grow moist. I was torn to bits by this tale of ardor in opposition to duty, and was unable to control my fits of sobbing. Peter squeezed my hand, assuming me to be a terribly sensitive soul. My crying jag became ungovernable, and I ran to the bathroom to bathe my face and eyes in cold compresses.

As I grabbed for a towel, I found myself staring at the gilded mermaids swimming at regular intervals across the black plastic shower curtain, and I remembered Esther Williams. She had been a mermaid in a film I had seen on television when I was about nine. I had desperately wanted to become a mermaid, too. The movie was sad, though. The mermaid was in love with a human; the affair was hopeless. Now, I buried my face in the towel, crying, "It's not fair!" and punching Peter's towel.

The following day, I was picked up by a man at the commute train station. I had never been picked up before, but I told myself that fellow stranded passengers were allowed to fraternize, and as we did not even leave the train station, it was not a true pick up.

I had been running for the 6:30 train, having missed the 5:45, crying over drinks with David. "Damn!" I hissed when I heard Gate 6 slam shut before I was halfway there.

"You, too?" a voice asked, and I looked sideways to glimpse a handsome young man in a very good trench coat. He was carrying a bag from John Walker and Company, Wine Merchants. "God, we just missed it," he complained.

"I've already missed the 5:45," I volunteered. Aren't you bold? I thought, wondering if the two glasses of red wine I drank with David were responsible for my willingness to chat up a strange man.

"Want to wait in there?" he asked, indicating "Ricky's Rendezvous," the bar in the train station.

I did not hesitate for a second. "Sure," I agreed. "We can wait there for the 7:30."

We both stopped at the phone booths. He explained he had a date on the Peninsula; she was to pick him up at the station. I told him I had to call my husband. I felt totally off the hook, then. I had placed it in the open right away that I was a married woman, not someone on the make.

We settled into one of those fat booths one finds in such places. I ordered a daiquiri, remembering that once my father had said that was what a "lady" should drink. My escort laughed at my order and said he would have one, too. The bartender brought them in plastic stemware, which we failed to notice in the pitch black of the bar. When we picked our glasses up with normal wrist action, liquid flew up out of our glasses and splashed onto our formica-topped table. We laughed, wiped up the mess with our tiny Ricky's Rendezvous paper napkins, clicked plastic together in a toast to the 7:30 train, and downed the unspilled portions of our drinks. The bartender brought us another round, with apologies. I was beginning to feel exceedingly festive. I realized at that moment that I had always wanted to drink out of plastic stemware in a dark seedy bar in a train station with a total stranger. I had learned since meeting David that once a person began doing things she thought she would never do, dozens of such things inevitably followed.

"My name's Dan," my gentleman friend told me.

"Vicky," I told him. I saw the bartender perk up. He had evidently assumed we knew each other, and the fact that we did not seemed to jog his interest. Perhaps this would be meatier stuff than the usual commuting men who patronized the bar and talked of sports and money. He moved along the bar, wiping it with a towel, until he was close enough to our table to be able to hear all that we were saying. I could see him better than he could see us, as the wall behind the bar was mirrored, giving me a reflected view of the back of him, as well as of myself and my gent. "Where do you live?" I asked Dan.

"San Diego. I'm just up here for a few days for my firm, and I have a date with a stewardess who lives in Burlingame. It's our first real date — I hope she's not too mad about me being late."

"Well, you telephoned, for godsake, it's not like you're a no-show, or something," I said. I sighed. "God, I live all the way down in Belmont. It's going to be 8:30 by the time I get home, now."

"Were you working today?"

"Yes, but I had a drink with a friend after work, and that's how I missed the 5:45 and 6:30 trains. I'd better not have another drink, because I had no lunch today and I'm starting to feel dizzy from the booze already."

"We can remedy that," he said, jumping up from his red leather seat. "Barman, another round, please," he requested, and to me, "I'll be right back." He returned laden with crackers, cheese, and a box of popcorn, all of which he had bought from a vendor in the station. My face felt deeply flushed from red wine and rum, and I tore into the popcorn with an abandon not customary in my approach to salty carbohydrates.

"You know what," I said, with an exaggerated, sentimental lilt already creeping into my speech. "I'm glad we missed the train. You're handsome and nice, and I always wanted to have a drink with such a beautiful raincoat."

"Will your husband be angry?" he inquired.

"I don't know," I said, waving away the question with a breezy motion of my hand. "He's used to me doing whatever I want."

"Really independent, and with freckles, too," he said, smiling. "I wish I didn't have to meet the stewardess."

We had made an unspoken pact to be best drinking buddies, and to flirt a bit too. We began talking animatedly to each other almost simultaneously, waving our arms, talking about our childhoods, launching off into territory not usually reached within a brief encounter. It seemed commuters could have true travelers' camaraderie, the way people on ocean voyages could. I began to suspect the bartender of going a little heavy on the rum; Dan and I were both suddenly so manic, and I could see the bartender smiling at our exchanges. I found the corny little colored lights over the bar suddenly terribly charming and not quite American. "Danny, do you love it when you're walking in the sun and the concrete is twinkling?"

"I love it, and I also love the huge reddish-brown dachshund heads they have outside of the Doggie Diners. Do you know they're getting rid of them?" he said somewhat loudly, banging his fist a bit on the table in a show of outrage.

"Let's kiss," I said.

"OK." We mingled tongues and laughed hysterically, and the bartender called out, "Two more daiquiris? I think I just heard the 7:30 leaving."

"Oh, no!" we screamed, "this is terrible," not stopping our laughter for a second. Dan ran out to the platform to make certain that the train had in fact departed. He came back shrugging and handed me a quarter. "Time for the second phone call," he said, and off we scurried to the booths.

"What did she say when you told her you missed the train again?" I asked when he came back to our booth.

"She said the soufflé fell," he said somberly. I howled.

"What'd he say?" he asked.

"He said, 'I see.'"

"Does he?"

I sighed. "He doesn't want to, Dan. I've tried to tell him about something that's happening to me, but his eyes just go blank and he changes the subject."

"Something, or somebody?" Dan inquired.

"Both." There was a longish silence. "But, one night after dinner we were listening to a Frank Zappa tape and talking, and he took a pencil in his hand, and with the eraser he traced the word 'cuckold' on his placemat."

"Cuckold? Does anybody really still use that word?"

"He's been fascinated by the word since he heard Marcello say it in one of his films," I explained. "And, when I asked him what in hell he was trying to say, he just smirked."

"God, all my friends are unhappily married," he said sadly.

"I'm not unhappy!" I insisted, and then, "Let's have a margarita for the road; I'm sick of these sissy drinks." The jukebox began playing "I

Left My Heart in San Francisco," and Dan and I loudly pretended to vomit. We knew we were officially bombed then. We ordered the tequila, anyway.

"You're coming with me tonight!" he announced. "We're going to go get on the 9:00, wait there in our top-decker seats, drink one of the bottles of cabernet I was taking her, and you're coming to dinner with us; she will understand."

"I don't want to go out with a man and a stewardess," I complained. Then, cheering up a bit, "But, we can drink the cabernet anyway, and you two can drink the other bottle in Burlingame."

We tipped the bartender lavishly and ran to the train; it was still dimly lighted and the heater was not yet on. We went to the top deck and took seats facing each other. Dan opened the red wine with the screw on his Swiss army knife and we poured it into the plastic glasses we were still clutching. "To us, to tonight, and to the 9 P.M.," Dan said, dramatically clicking his glass against mine and sending red wine down the front of both of us.

Tears were spilling, too, bouncing off my bosom and splashing about. Dan was sloshed. "What's wrong, darling gardenia, my pet?" he asked, eyes large and mouth turned sadly down.

"When you," I gulped, "when you get old, your earlobes keep growing."

"And so?" he asked, swilling a huge glass of red. His lower lip was stained with wine.

"And so," I said, "and so, they get really big. They're absolutely hideous. Haven't you noticed them on old people?"

He shrugged a bit.

"They hang way down. It's grotesque. And the old ladies wear horrid big earrings on their massive earlobes, and it's awful." My tears were fierce. "I'm getting mine hacked off if they get big," I announced.

"There, there, darling," he said, and we began laughing again, sputtering, and stomping our feet a bit too, until some of the men-with-briefcases on the lower deck glared at us.

We quieted down as much as we could, and soon the train was

pulling out of the station. We cheered. "We made it!" Dan exulted. "I was beginning to think we weren't destined to reach the Peninsula."

"I knew we'd make it, old boy," I said, "but I was afraid it might be on the 10:50."

On the way home, he asked me what I liked to do, and I told him I liked to see old films. He told me his favorite of all times was *The Magnificent Seven*. I told him mine was called *One Touch of Venus*, which had starred Ava Gardner. I explained that Ava played a department store mannequin that magically came alive after the store closed. She stood frozen and stony all day on a plastic pedestal, but at night she turned into a human and carried on a romance with a young man who worked in the store.

He said, "You mean every time they got it on, she'd just turn back into a dummy in the morning?" and refilled his glass. "How decent of her."

"It was sad," I said. "Their love was doomed."

"Life often imitates art," Dan muttered, but he was so drunk it sounded as if he had said, "Wife often imitates art."

"Art who?" I responded, and held out my glass for more.

It seemed as if only five minutes had passed before the wine was gone and Dan was bolting down the steps to the lower deck and disembarking in Burlingame. "Ciao-ciao, bambina!" he called to me, tucking the scrap of paper with my false phone number on it into his breast pocket and waving jauntily. Belmont loomed up very soon, and I detrained and walked up the hill to my apartment. I looked up at the window and sighed, feeling dizzy and slightly nauseated from the booze. Walking in, I heard the same Zappa tape playing that we had been listening to when Peter wrote "cuckold" on his placemat. The cut "Weasels Ripped My Flesh" was throwing out white noise. Peter appeared in the doorway with a tight jaw. "Glad you could make it," he said.

"Don't mention it," I said, tossing my coat onto a chair.

"What the hell is that?" he demanded, pointing to my hand.

Looking down, I saw that I was still holding on to the plastic glass.

Some salt remained around the rim from the margarita, and it was stained red from the wine.

"I had a drink on the way home," I told him. "I'm sorry I'm late." Stopping, I put my hand on his arm, saying, "Really, Peter, I truly am terribly sorry," and I headed for the bathroom.

In the bathroom, I did not turn on the light, but stood there in the darkness, feeling sick from more than the liquor. I could not see Esther Williams, but I knew she was there.

endings

She and Phillip play the odd sort of game they always play for the first hour. They circle around each other; move in close to each other; she goes into the kitchen, into the bathroom, acts aloof — busy. Then they have a drink together, chat and smile a lot like a potential couple in a singles bar. After forty-five minutes of the game, he says, "Come here," and softly taps the place next to him on the sofa. The dog rushes to the sofa instead.

When she does go sit by Phillip, she touches his hair and they both laugh intemperately, exchanging glances that say, "Isn't it amusing the way we stalk each other in the beginning?" Then, as always, they kiss, the dog moaning with jealousy.

Her entire body turns to neon, smokes blue and red, flashes on and off. He apparently cannot breathe, is choked by ardor, and she resolves to make him quit smoking. They kiss, writhe, throw clothing in all directions, taste everything, have each other roughly, murmuring, "Baby, darling, I love you, I love you," biting each other to bits. She says, "Not where it shows," and bites him where it shows. Their own breath is so loud that neither of them hears her husband's key in the door. He is suddenly just there, and they are caught like two dogs stuck together in the street, dogs who need to be drenched by the garden hose in order to be pulled apart.

She and Phillip are both wearing their glasses. They look more studious than passionate as they hunch over the newspaper together.

He is smiling because Dear Abby is trying to sound Zen again. She is scowling over the parole of a local rapist. They hear the door open and they sit ramrod straight, looking at each other with an "Oh my god!" look, then with a "break-a-leg" look two actors might exchange before going onstage.

"Darling, this is Bud, from the office," she chirps, face purple. Face neon red and blue, blinking on and off.

"How do you do," Phillip says, standing to shake hands. She is grateful he has not said, "Nice to meet ya'." In the end, it does not matter what he says, because her husband looks at them both as if they are excrement and he silently exits.

Phillip brings her flowers. He is a child about flowers. He brings her hand-picked ones, sticking them into her mailbox when she is not home, or, as today, brings her a motley bouquet, while she would never Mix Her Flowers. She always buys twelve white roses or eighteen yellow button flowers; he buys bushy, hairy-stalked bunches of flowers, no two the same. She loves him for it, is vanquished by it, loves the contrast between Phillip's somewhat sinister side and his fresh-faced, Norman Rockwell side.

She is putting the flowers into a vase and watching Phillip help himself to her husband's brandy when she hears the Jaguar prematurely in the driveway. A premature Jag, flashing red and blue neon.

"Hide in the basement!" she screams at Phillip, and she thinks of the time she found an empty sherry glass in the morning on the table, covered with fuzzy black ants.

Phillip books a room in one of the city's finest hotels for their anniversary. They know they will have only a few hours together, that they will have to rush through the French dinner before they go upstairs, but they have learned to live with that during the two years they have been meeting. Two years of sin; she hates herself for that, but rushes toward the downtown hotel with a smile on her flushed face — two years of darling, darling Phillip. The sun has just gone down and the neon sign over the new brasserie on the square seems to be there just for her and Phillip, the red and blue merging into a smoldering purple. She is weighted down by her large red shoulder bag, overstuffed with clean underwear and all her makeup — weighted down too by the oversized rectangular box she is clutching. She has bought Phillip a new comforter for his bed, an anniversary present she knows they will both enjoy. The comforter now on his bed has a cigarette burn on it, and she has always thought she smells the perfume of women past in the fabric. He is waiting for her in the lobby, jumps up with a joyful face when he sees her, taking the box from her arms and juggling it with the bottle of champagne he carries in a thin white paper bag with a silver-cord handle.

"Happy number two, baby doll," he says, and she slips her arm through his, caressing his sleeve.

"Baby doll?" a cruel voice asks. They turn in unison to see her husband standing there. Phillip recognizes him immediately from photographs; she does not recognize him in the first instant.

"I saw you on the street and followed you in," her husband tells her, face graying rapidly. "At least it's not a cheap hotel," he says, one side of his mouth turning down in a sardonic snarl. He is out the revolving door and gone before she and Phillip move at all.

They are at Phillip's apartment this time. It is the only place she ever feels safe with him. She knows meeting at her house is insanity, and that she could always be seen entering or leaving a hotel. Phillip's apartment seems totally safe and cozy. But it is forty miles from her house. Forty miles from the school where she picks up her son in late afternoon.

She is sitting up in Phillip's bed, sipping a glass of coffee brandy and rubbing away the smeared mascara from under her eyes. They have both been crying, but Phillip's tears did not leave black tracks on his face. She began sobbing when they were twenty minutes into the sex, and then they both ended up crying, saying, "What are we going to *do?*" and clutching each other like waifs.

Phillip is basting the turkey. Because they have never spent a holiday together, they are pretending it is Thanksgiving. She has baked a pumpkin pie, doing so when her husband took their little boy to a football game and then hiding the pie in the back of her car. She brings the pie and wine and brie, he cooks the turkey dinner. She has found a papier-mâché turkey with a gold crown on its head in a junk shop and brings it for a centerpiece. She wonders if they should say grace. What would she pray at the dinner table with Phillip? Dear Father, we thank you for this food, we thank you for this scorchy neon love, cooking the turkey without an oven, forgive us our sins, amen.

"Don't cry, pet," he says, pulling back the sheet and looking at her belly as if he is ready to baste it, too. "This is the first of many thanks giving days," and he begins feasting.

The knock on the door is only a slight annoyance—a fly to be brushed off; they are already far away.

"Open up!" a distorted voice demands.

They stumble from the bed, groping for robes, and he parts the bedroom curtains to peer outside.

Her husband's red Jaguar is parked at the curb.

She drives to the supermarket in a grump. The day is unseasonably hot; she is dripping and flustered, driving with all the windows open wide. She sticks to the red fake-leather upholstery, clothes and brow wrinkled. She parks the car sloppily and grabs for her purse on the scorching seat beside her. She is thinking about the hobo she saw in front of the dry cleaners. He said, "Hey, Sis—I'm eleven cents short—will you help me out?" She looked at him—amiable, honest face, bunched-up wool ski cap in the ninety-degree heat—and said yes, fumbling in her purse and handing him a dollar. His face was as ecstatically shocked as if she had handed him a hundred dollars, and he held the bill at arm's length, face transfigured by surprise, saying, "Oh my god!" and holding his arms out like a fisherman who had let one get away.

She is smiling slightly at the remembrance as she begins to roll up the window. The horror quickly fills up the left side of her peripheral vision; a man putting his head through the open window of her car. Her gasp is so loud it frightens her: She has always known this would happen, has always driven with the door locked and the windows rolled up. His tongue is down her throat, then it is sliding along her gums, pushing hotly beneath her top lip, then over the space where her wisdom teeth used to be — it is everywhere at once. There was no question as to who it was from his tongue's first impact, from the first sweaty clutching of her neck. She was still squeaking and shaking in fear at the beginning of the kiss, but then her mouth opened soakingly all the way to receive Philip, though she slapped him sharply once on the face, shouting a muffled, "Damn you!" through the kiss.

"Babe, sweetest, I couldn't stand it any longer," he is saying, sucking her neck from outside the car and knocking her sunglasses off.

She looks at him with insincere harshness, phony austerity. "You idiot, Phillip," she says, her voice too soft, an Ivory soap voice. She looks into his blue-green eyes — they are neon signs flashing: "You Know What You Want" and she blinks the vision away, saying, "God, Phillip — do you know what that kiss was like?" She notices he has a suntan. "It was like those little orange plastic containers we used to get at the movies — shaped like oranges and full of orange juice, and we used to just *squeeze* the juice into our mouths and *die*."

"You're coming with me," he says, pulling the keys from the ignition and putting them into his back pocket.

"Don't be a fool," she says in a stranger's voice, sweat beading on her upper lip, dripping between her breasts. She says to herself a mantra, "I am a mother, my son loves and needs me."

His hand is down her back, he is leading her to his car.

"This time you're not going back," he tells her.

She marries him. No — he disgraces her. She goes to live with him and then he rejects her. She has nobody. No — they live happily ever after, flashing red and blue, neon, neon, into eternity. But really:

She loses her family, her prestige, her security. He takes advantage of her, drags her into the gutter. They are blissful together, they have a baby — they are so in love they forget how stupid it is to have babies. In fact, she is too old to want babies again, and he is too wise to think he would be any sort of a father. They have a cute little home; she teaches him how to live well. They live shabbily and messily; she forgets about being a respectable woman. She loses her son, loses her parents. No — he gains a child, his parents adore her. For years afterward, she tells people that when she and Phillip met, she was living a sterile existence in a meaningless marriage, that Phillip had set her life ablaze, flashing blue and red neon, hot and right, putting his smoking brand on her flank. He lies to her, cheats on her, leaves her a poor woman in a world of material goods. He saves her from narcolepsy, loves her until she forgets her identity as an unloved person; he scorches the edges of her life, high-voltage.

shadow boxing

"Have you ever noticed there's no such thing as a chicken omelette?" Phillip asked.

"Chicken liver omelettes—yes there are," Victoria said, drinking down her second Ramos Fizz and thinking about *The Great Gatsby*. The carton of eggs they brought with them to the bar that morning was sitting near her left elbow, three of its oval-shaped cavities empty.

"I think it's considered a form of cannibalism," he continued. "I've eaten in many omelette houses, and never once have I seen an actual chicken omelette. It seems to be sort of taboo."

"You mean eating the chickens and their offspring at the same time?" she asked, nodding as the bartender asked if they wanted another round of fizzes. "It would only be cannibalism if the chickens were eating the eggs."

Phillip pushed the carton toward the bartender again so she could take another egg for the drinks. She was named Vicky, they learned. She was an elderly woman with a blonde wig and false eyelashes, very kindly. Victoria said with a wide smile, "Oh, we have the same name!" but felt her heart sink.

Phillip dropped a handful of coins into the jukebox. Rock music blared forth and he motioned to her that he would like to dance.

"Not now, darling," Victoria told Phillip. She thought she was not quite drunk enough, yet, to dance at a neighborhood alcoholics' bar at nine in the morning.

The old-timers, regulars in The Shadow Box bar every morning at eight o'clock gave them angry looks. This younger couple had invaded the morning routine with their carton of eggs, their fizzes, and their music. The pair telephoned before arriving, asking if they could get fizzes there, and Vicky the bartender said she had no eggs. Twenty minutes later, they came in laughing with their egg carton. The regulars were accustomed to scotch "neat," talk of the morning sports page, and flirting with old Vicky, having her undivided attention.

Phillip sat again on the stool next to her, encircling her waist with his arm and thanking the older Vicky for the fizzes, giving her a flashy smile. Victoria noticed the barmaid blushed as Phillip smiled at her, her stiff black eyelashes fluttered like Bambi's. She wondered if they were made of real hair.

"I love you," he whispered into Victoria's ear, his face flushed. Only an hour before, they were both grouchy and pale, she with a throbbing headache, wearing sunglasses, the light like a knife.

"Remember *The Great Gatsby?*" she said. "The part about Egg Harbor?" She could not decide whether her heart was pounding from the gin or from Phillip's breath in her ear. "There was a billboard of some kind, something about an egg, do you remember?"

"Actually, I do," Phillip said, leaning closer into her face. "It was a billboard with an eye doctor's advertisement on it. Dr. Something-or-Other, gigantic eyeglasses."

"I remember that now," she said. "Was it Egg Harbor?" She could have sworn there had been an egg on the billboard itself, or a bald head like an egg.

"I think it was a place called West Egg," Phillip said. He burned her cheek with a kiss. "But I do remember that the eyes on the billboard were as huge and blue and terrifying as yours."

"Terrified, you mean," she responded, but he did not hear her. He had pulled her up, moving to the beat of the record. He took her hand and led her toward the back of the bar near the pool table, where they could dance.

"You kids must be feeling better," the bartender called out to them, laughing. They laughed, too, at the word "kids." The woman said it was nice to see someone dancing for a change. The regulars ignored them.

"Promise you'll make me a chicken omelette, after," Victoria said, dancing with abandon in The Shadow Box, face bubble-gum-pink from the gin. Gin in a frothy white brew, just like a milkshake, gin and eggs, beautiful gin long before noon, gorgeous Phillip. She was sorry she had balked at coming in, calling it a "bum's bar" and pouting in the car while Phillip bought the eggs at the Eazy Mart. Lovely gin and eggs.

Her head was pounding again. One hand shaded her eyes when David turned on the light, and the book she had been reading earlier fell to the floor. She had been asleep on the sofa, exhausted from the day with Phillip, exhausted from all of it.

David was late, stuck at the office until after nine. Carlo was already sleeping soundly in his bed built to resemble a truck. David made it for him when he outgrew the crib.

"Have you eaten?" he asked, as she sat up, blinking.

"No, I just gave Carlo a hamburger — I wasn't really hungry and didn't know if you would have eaten or not."

"How 'bout I make us scrambled eggs?" David suggested. "I'm not all that hungry either, and I could stir some of the leftover Chinese food into the eggs."

"Good, thanks," she said. She hoped she had already fully digested the chicken and avocado omelette Phillip made after they got out of bed. No one in her family had ever died of heart disease.

David stopped in the hallway and asked, "Are you all right?" with a critical edge to his voice.

"I'm fine, just tired, with a bit of a headache again," she told him, getting up and looking for her shoes.

"Couldn't you do something about your car?" he said, then, standing very still in the hallway. She could not see his expression because of the glare from the light.

"Like what?" she asked, trying to remember that unpleasantness never helped.

"It's filthy," he said, and she laughed. "I just moved it across the street for you — you were going to get a ticket in the morning. Tomorrow is a street-cleaning day."

She said nothing, but the thought, "I have a filthy car," created a hysteria centered somewhere between her breasts and her navel. It fluttered, pushed, she was going to start laughing and not be able to stop. My car is filthy. She was biting her lip.

David's voice was strained, accusative. "When I opened the car door, some tampons fell out into the street."

"Oh my god," she said, frowning, crossing her legs tightly as she sat down again, trying not to be a child.

She had told Dr. Feldman that as a little girl she often fantasized about throwing food at her parents during dinner. That she sat demurely, saying nothing, listening to their verbal assaults, dreamy eyed, visualizing herself picking up her plate of dried-out roast beef and salad with plain mayo as dressing and heaving it brutally into the face of her mother or father. She confessed, too, that only a few weeks ago she had flung herself onto the king-sized bed she shared with her husband, closed her eyes, and imagined herself throwing eggs at him. A dozen. One by one, eggs hitting his forehead with a thud and then oozing all over him. Bouncing off the walls, white shells everywhere, goo on the floor, David putting his hands up in self-defense and shouting, "What the hell are you doing?"

"I'll clean it out tomorrow," she said quietly. She relished the image of a white-paper-wrapped tampon falling out of the car and rolling down the hill.

"How did the meeting go?" she asked him, following him into the kitchen. His shoulders seemed stooped, smaller than they used to be. She poured two gin and tonics, handed him one as he opened the wire-handled Chinese food take-out box.

"It was a bitch," he said. "What about you? What did you do today?"

I drank gin and danced at 9 A.M. in a neighborhood bar near my lover's apartment. Danced, then left, our arms around each other. We made love in his bed for five hours, lost track of time, laughing and crying, we can both barely walk now. We were so electrified you could have fried an egg on us. We had an omelette with the eggs left over from the fizzes, a chicken omelette.

"Not much. Went into the office this morning for a few hours, then shopped around." She watched David breaking the eggs for scrambling. She wanted eggs. The smoothness, ovalness, noncomplexity of eggs, the purity. She knew she was the opposite of an egg—her car was filthy.

She was amazed to see that when she glanced down at the newspaper David had brought home with him, the following line appeared in the column full of trivia items: "Lumberjacks estimate by rings in wood that eggs found in a tree at Klamath falls have been there for a hundred years."

"Marry me," Phillip said, his voice expressionless.

"How romantic," she responded. "Takes a lot of passion to propose to a married woman."

He turned his dark head toward her on the pillow they shared, frowned and puffed his cigarette noisily. "People get divorced," he said. "When they love someone else."

She sat up and refilled their champagne glasses from the bottle of Mumm's on Phillip's nightstand. "You don't want to get married, Phillip," she said, hoping he did not.

"I do now," he said. "I changed my mind." He looked at her from over the rim of his own glass, stern green eyes, sizing her up.

They heard someone crying upstairs, wailing, "Oh, no, no, no. No, no no," sobbing loudly.

"The two gay guys in the apartment upstairs," Phillip explained. "Their cat died this morning."

"God, how awful," she said. "How awful and pitiful and sad." Tears welled up in her eyes.

"So you won't?"

"Can't." She put her head on his chest. He always smelled like baking bread, his smell followed her wherever she went. She must never let him know that she would leave everyone, everything, follow him to the crummiest, most sordid corner of the world. Which was where he would take her, she knew.

"You can't fool me. I know you love me." His voice lost its dreamy quality, then, and he said, "God, I do get sick of chasing you, though. Especially when you jump out of the car or run out the front door and I have to sprint after you. I must have chased you a thousand times, pulled you out of bushes, dragged you off the steps of buses — it's ridiculous."

"Six hundred times," she said, listening to the crying of the man with a dead cat. Would they put the corpse in the garbage can out in front, or would they call someone to take it away?

"What?" Philip lit another cigarette with annoyance, looking at her the way David sometimes did.

"You've only chased me down six hundred times," she told him. "When you've done it a thousand times, we can get married."

"It's because I'm not well-heeled and upwardly mobile like your husband," he said. It was odd to see Phillip with an impassive face — he, usually so animated.

In a cruel monotone she said, "It's because we both drink too much, because you work as a stage magician and I can't follow you around from town to town, gig to gig. It's because you will always gamble away everything either of us earns, because I'm eight years older than you, because I have a little boy and a husband, because when we're together we forget what real life is."

"What is real life, older, smarter one?" Phillip demanded. He remembered to touch her so she would forget the answer.

Real life is not magic tricks and magnums of champagne, Phillip — not you and I. Not you and I, in the dark, hearing wind whooshing past our ears, or is it someone whispering? Whispering secrets.

She was strong for a few moments, answered him before sinking beneath the waves.

"Real life is hangovers, dead cats, and deceit."

He would not listen, said, "Don't you want something else for us? Don't you want us to be able to do something together other than drink, eat, and go to bed?"

"I'd like us to quit eating."

"Good at distracting the audience, aren't you?" he said, looking older. "I should use you as a shill for my act — need a little part-time work?"

"I'd rather be the woman you saw in half," Victoria said, closing her eyes. Closing her ears against the cries of the man upstairs.

She did not drink anything during the last two hours she spent with Phillip. She was afraid to drink right before she picked Carlo up from school. Her friend Sheila said to her one day, "I never drink at lunch when I'm going to be picking Megan up at nursery school — I'm afraid I'll get into a car crash and kill her." Victoria knew that Sheila meant this for her, meant, "For godsake Vicky, don't pick up Carlo when you're tanked."

She said to her little boy, "You sure got dirty today. Were you playing soccer after class?" He tossed his books aside and fastened his seat belt, knowing she would not turn on the engine until he did.

Instead of answering her, Carlo asked, "Is there really a God?"

"No one knows," she answered. "Everyone has their own god."

"If he *is* around, can he see you all the time? Does God see everything?" Carlo asked.

"Well, yes, he would," she said, feeling it was she who should be asking these questions.

"Then I don't like him," Carlo said. "I don't want anyone looking at me all the time."

"Nor I, that's for sure," she agreed.

"Will Daddy be home for dinner?"

"No, Daddy will be playing tennis at the club this evening," she said. *Daddy will be playing with his girlfriend, and it will not be at the tennis club.*

She was not listening to Carlo anymore, was driving the car like an automaton, staring ahead, not thinking about what she was doing, just somehow making it home on automatic pilot while she thought about David. David, whom she once loved so passionately it sometimes embarrassed their friends. David, who was so romantic he carried her over the threshold of the hotel on their honeymoon, who called her Vicky-love and Sweetie-pie and who used to lunch with her three times a week even though his professional schedule was hectic. He who had devastated her by being unfaithful to her, nearly ten years into their marriage. She had sobbed on and on, "Oh, no no, no no."

"Kevin says God sees everything. Says he sees you when you undress, even," Carlo told her.

"Don't worry about God, Carlo. Just worry about the people you know exist. Today, just worry about getting your homework done, OK?"

As soon as he was in the bathtub, she could collapse on the sofa with a huge gin-soda, no ice. And it would happen then, as it always did. The tuning out and the tuning in. She would tune out the pain, tune out the urge to scream. Tune in the wild hot burning sensation from forehead to groin, tune in the feeling that she was invincible, savage and witty and happy. Feel that way until she later fell asleep, another day behind her.

"I'll tell you something, Carlo," she confessed to her son. "When I was a girl, I was worried, too, about God seeing me undress. I was so upset about it I tore up a picture of Jesus that my mother had put on my bedroom wall. I thought the eyes might be staring at me."

"Oh, Mommy, you're really bad!" Carlo said, giggling, face shining pink with delight. "That's even worse than when you lied and told Uncle Bart he was adopted."

"Yep," she said. "God's gonna get me if I don't watch out."

"Good morning, Sweetie-pie," David said, tousling her hair from beside her in their bed. He had come in late, she knew. She heard him tiptoeing upstairs in the night and glanced at the clock before pretending to be asleep; it was nearly three.

"Did you have a nice time last night?" she asked him, feeling neutral, platonic, hoping David actually did have a good time.

"It was OK," he said noncommittally. "What on earth are you wearing?" He pulled the covers down and laughed. "This isn't Halloween, Vicky — what is that get-up?"

He was smiling, amused and lighthearted. She noticed he still had beautiful, straight white teeth.

"Well, I fell asleep on the sofa with my clothes on last night," she admitted, laughing herself. "I woke up about midnight and came to bed, and I guess I was only half undressed."

She was wearing a bright pink camisole over a black bra, a pair of black-and-white striped underpants and black-and-white checkered knee-socks. "It's sort of strange sleeping with socks on," she told him, thinking the hangover was not that bad.

"You look like a French carousel figure," David said.

She noticed, though, that when she arose and looked into the full-length mirror on the bedroom wall, she looked like a French carousel figure who had been savagely beaten. She had neglected to wash off her eye makeup, and the black mascara and liner were badly smudged.

"I look like I have two shiners," she said. "Bring on the beefsteak." But she thought of a couple she had seen coming into The Shadow Box bar the morning she was there with Phillip. Just as she and Phillip rose to leave, they had come through the swinging doors, lighting the room with the brightness of the morning. The man was probably in his forties, the woman obviously much younger, though weathered and worn for her age. Both of them wore polyester slacks and "Go 49ers" sweatshirts. They were joking with each other as they came in. Their faces were equally red, bloated, and puffy; it was apparent they spent a lot of mornings in The Shadow Box. The woman had two black eyes of such magnitude that Phillip and Victoria quickly looked away. She looked like a quarterback with paint under her eyes, or like a bulldog with two black circles. The man and woman seemed so happy together, and yet it was somehow clear that he had blackened her eyes.

"You really shouldn't drink so much, you know that, Vicky?" David said from the bed, his voice subdued.

"Yes, I know," she answered, rubbing the black from her eyes with some cold cream she kept on the bureau top. Heading toward the shower, she said, "I'll quit drinking if it gets out of hand."

In the shower, she made a mental list of her options. Humming a disconnected tune, she thought, David and I will get counseling, I'll go to A.A./I'll join a cult—find a cult where they all hug me a lot/I'll quit my job, leave David, and go to Las Vegas with Phillip, and send for Carlo later/I will drink myself to death—what a way to go.

There was a sudden sharp noise and Victoria stopped dreaming her list. "Oh!" she exclaimed, startled. The sound was a clackety rattling, like a noisy skeleton. Her heart raced for a moment and then she realized what it was. Carlo's wind-up toy aqua-man, resting on the shower caddy, had suddenly begun swimming by itself. Out of water, he made a fearful racket as he swam in place, his orange plastic arms circling and his thin legs kicking the metal on the shower caddy. He wore a set of black air tanks. He swam on the caddy for perhaps six seconds, then gave up, resigning himself to being wound-down and trapped on the shelf. She picked him up and looked at his molded plastic head. The diving headgear made him look bald—he resembled a fetus. His eyes were pulled back in a panicky, stretch-lidded way, there was only a hole for a mouth. She looked at his face, captivated, stared into the little round hole of a mouth, gazed directly into his very head. His face appeared agonized.

in season

Victoria begins expecting Phillip on Thanksgiving Day, is so nervous she forgets to cook the yams, burns the rolls, and bursts into tears in front of her husband and in-laws.

She has heard nothing from him since he sent a postcard to her office in early November, six days after checking out of the hospital and going to Las Vegas without a goodbye. The note said only, "I'm coming for you. If you think about it, you'll know when to expect me."

She anticipates his reappearance on every holiday. He makes his moves on holidays: They met on New Year's Eve, had their first lovers' quarrel on his birthday. He asked her to run away with him on the Fourth of July, tried to hang himself on Halloween.

Thanksgiving ends quietly with no sign of Phillip.

David is snoring softly on the sofa, Victoria chewing solitarily on a cold turkey drumstick, imagining Phillip enjoying Thanksgiving with another woman.

She examines the entertainment section of the Sunday newspaper very carefully each week to see whether "Phillip Zanzibar, Black Magic and Stage Illusions" appears as second billing in an afternoon show at one of the Vegas casinos, but she never sees his name.

Phillip habitually avoids Hanukkah and ignores Christmas, so it is not until New Year's that Victoria begins again to expect him.

She and David leave Carlo with her parents for the weekend and drive to a hotel near the ocean. They dine in an elegant restaurant on New Year's Eve. David is a stunning stranger in his tux; Victoria bares

149

her shoulders, shows some cleavage. They eat paté, drink champagne, and out of the corner of her eye she watches for Phillip. She sees a man drinking alone in a corner of the hotel bar. He wears very dark glasses in the dim light of the bar and has the body of a born lover. She looks hard, but it is not Phillip's smile that lights up the man's face as she stares at him.

Phillip telephones her from somewhere else. His timing is excellent. He knows where she is, just as he always has. He has even telephoned her in the past at her hairdresser's, though she never mentioned Mr. Lucio's salon to him. Now, she is three steps into the women's lounge before the page calls, "Victoria Zack, to a blue phone, please, Victoria Zack." Though her married name is Wright. Though David will hear it too, and wonder.

"Yes?" she says into the powder blue telephone, restraining herself from saying, "Yes, Phillip."

"Viva Las Vegas," he says.

The mauve carpet on the floor seems to be shifting, slipping away like sand from under her feet.

"Did you see that film?" she asks, and it is as if two hours have passed since the last time they spoke, not two months.

"I'm too young to appreciate Elvis, remember?" he says.

"Phillip," she tells him, "I thought you weren't coming back."

"No, you didn't," he says. "Are you coming with me?"

"You're crazy," she says, voice icy, denying. "You should have stayed in the loony bin," and she hangs up, knowing she is setting up another test, spurring him on.

If you want to be Rasputin, she thinks, you are going to have to work harder at it.

When she returns to the table, it is clear David has not heard the page for Victoria Zack. Perhaps he is oblivious to her maiden name after all these years.

Phillip telephones her house later that week. "I just want to say hello," he lies.

She tells him *that* will be the day. "Just get out of my life," she says in a gangster's voice.

And, while you are getting out of my life, get out of my dreams, out of my marriage, out of my mind. Go marry someone, out of my life. But don't you dare, don't even think about it, don't have a Jewish wedding and go to Rio on your honeymoon. You were going to let me break the glass with my foot, and I was going to show you the Christ on the hill when we flew into Rio de Janeiro.

But she does not say any of these things, says instead, "Get out of my life."

Martin Luther King's photograph appears on the front page of the newspaper, but Victoria does not have the day off as a holiday. Carlo's school is closed for the day, so she takes him to daycare and goes to the office as usual. When she arrives at work, there is a huge balloon-bouquet floating above her desk. Twenty gaudy helium balloons. The card says simply, "I have a dream."

She despises balloon clusters, finds them vulgar. Phillip would know this about her instinctively. She has often felt sorry for someone when one of the young, tuxedoed delivery boys showed up with a gigantic group of balloons, calling everyone's attention to the recipient. It is humiliating for her now to receive one of the oversized greetings, to sit beneath the hovering mass like a kid in a dunce cap.

She cannot get rid of them. They are too big to throw away. It would create a bigger disturbance at the office to try and ditch a floating island of balloons than to simply sit beneath them, thinking obsessively of Phillip's "dream." The balloons hover over her all day, moving slightly, constantly catching her eye, rubbing against each other, rubbing against her when she walks by. It seems one always brushes against her breast.

She recalls the time she came home to find a vase of roses in the house with an unsigned note from Phillip. The note said: "I know what you and Hubby are up to." It was the week before she reconciled with David.

She has not figured out how Phillip got into the house to deliver the flowers and the note. His being a stage conjurer does not seem a good enough explanation. The house has a locked gate and deadbolts on the front and back doors. Could he have been devious enough to press her house keys to a piece of clay and have keys made for himself?

Still, she thinks, chest constricting, he would not enter the house now that David is back home, even though it is Valentine's Day. It is only her body he demands entrance to, David or no David, no matter how many times she says no, means maybe.

I'll fake him out this time, she thinks. I will tell him yes and mean no, for a change. I will say, Yes, Phillip, any time you say—I give up, and he will lose interest, stand me up, leave me in the lurch.

Valentine's Day is too corny for Phillip, anyway, she decides.

When there is no valentine for her in the office mail, though, she feels herself blanch, then flush, her knees go rubbery. She wishes she had talked with Phillip when he telephoned, asked him where he lives now. She has cut herself off from him, cannot telephone him in a weak moment, run to his doorstep and say, "Darling, I'm here."

David sends intensely red tulips, fragile and sensual blooms on fat long stalks. He has always been gallant on Valentine's Day, bringing flowers or making funny cards for her. Earlier, she gave him a card, brought out heart-shaped pastries for Carlo and him for breakfast. But David is distant. Since they have been back together, she is amazed at how seldom he talks to her, how bored he looks when she talks to him. Was it always this way, even before his affair and their separation?

She tries not to blame David for being aloof; she blames herself, instead, knowing she has a tendency to smother people, demand intimacy to a crazy degree.

After Phillip, David seems cold, though, and stiff as cardboard. He has a nervous cough that hacks out every time he is irritated. When she asks him why he is coughing, he glares at her and tells her he has a cold.

He has begun to leave the toilet seat up last thing at night, so that if she gets up in the dark to go to the bathroom, she falls in. Often, he does not flush the toilet, either. She mentions this to her friend Jennifer who tells her it is passive-aggressive behavior.

When she leaves the office that evening, she thinks that maybe she will surprise David, take him out to a really nice dinner in a romantic restaurant for Valentine's Day. Perhaps she has not been demonstrative enough with him. Maybe he looks at his watch all the time because she really is boring.

She is startled when she gets into the car. There is a bird there; it flaps its wings against the side of its cage when she opens the door. It is big and white, a dove, she guesses. Phillip always used doves in his act.

What on earth am I supposed to do with it? If I set it free, will it die?

The creature's chest heaves, it is frightened, and Victoria tells it, "It's OK, I won't hurt you. I'll get you some nice seed, something sweet, too — a Valentine's treat." There is a card taped to the side of the cage; it is as white as the bird. Inside, one sentence only: "For Victoria: a bird in a gilded cage."

Would it be immoral to give the bird to David for Valentine's Day?

She has her arms full of blue-paper-wrapped shirts, starched and stacked. Hangers with dry-cleaned items are draped over her left arm. She sees him lounging on the hood of her car, lying in wait. She would know the arrogant posture anywhere.

"Phillip!" she shouts, running to the car, dropping one package of David's clean shirts onto the gravel, hearing the paper tear.

Phillip is wearing a large green button that says, "Kiss Me — I'm Irish."

"You're Jewish," she says, dropping all the laundry, now, throwing the hangers full of plastic-wrapped dresses to the ground so she can put her arms around Phillip.

"You're Irish," he says, "So it's OK," and they are kissing and she remembers there is no mouth in the world like his, never was, never will be. She does not care about the clothes, the passersby, her scruples, her morals, or anyone in the world but Phillip. She can feel that he will be her lover again, very soon, within a few minutes, even if it has to be in the car. The back seat folds down.

They stop kissing and Phillip picks up the clothes and puts them in the back of the car. The two of them slide into the front seat and she says, "Where on earth have you been? Why did you go to Las Vegas without telling me? Do you know what I've been through?"

"I had to earn enough money to be able to spirit you away," he says, and she tries to stop kissing his warm pink mouth because she wants to hear what he has to say for himself.

"I've been gambling—we can go to Rio after all," he says. "What did you do with the bird?"

"I donated it to Carlo's school for their fund-raising auction. I wanted to keep the cage, but of course I couldn't."

"Mrs. Wright," he says. "That's a good one, huh?" and his hand slips underneath her skirt, grazes her thigh. "Will you change your name when we're married?"

This is what she always thinks of as "the blitz." Phillip touches her and she feels as if she is sitting on a radiator. Then her mind goes and she says anything at all, babbles, becomes someone she has never met.

"Yes," she says, crazy, eyes glazing over.

"Yes, what?" he asks.

"Yes, I'll be Victoria Shapiro, or Zanzibar, or go back to my maiden name, or . . ."

" . . . and you *will* leave David and marry me and go to Rio for our honeymoon."

"Yes, yes, I'll iron your shirts, learn to make matzos," she says, and her forehead is hotter than a steam iron and is throbbing.

"You've been *bad,*" Phillip says. He is enjoying this, pinches her hard, high on the thigh and she squirms.

"Yes," she agrees. "Very bad," and for one quick laser beam of a second, she thinks, how in god's name did this happen to me? I am wild about a madman.

He tells her he has bought into the very same time-share condo she and David have at the lake, and when she gasps, he tells he now rents an apartment that is only two blocks from her house.

"It has a Murphy bed," he says. "How's that for St. Patrick's Day?"

She shoves the key into the ignition, but he directs her to an Irish bar, packed with rowdy celebrants. They drink green beer for an hour. He makes her wait.

tooth and nail

I saw Phillip's sister Lenore last Sunday night at the family party. Her smile reminded me of the grille of an old Buick, except mean. She said to me in a loud, cocktail-party voice, "Isn't it great that you and Phillip can go out in public together now — meet each other's friends, do normal things? No more sneaking around?"

I said, "I preferred sneaking around," and took a cool drink from my martini glass.

Lenore forced a false, "Ha, ha, ha," and said, "You're so funny, dear," though she is ten years younger than I. I looked into her very fat face, thought that somehow all fat people have the same face, but I knew I could not say so, even to Phillip. They call fat women "big" now, have special stores for them with names like "Big and Beautiful" and "The Forgotten Woman."

I felt fat, too, because of my period, and I stared at Lenore, thinking that Phillip told me she injects herself in the rear end every day with something from a vial she keeps in the refrigerator. It says "PMS Clinic," and she shakes it up each morning after coffee and goes into the bathroom with it. Phillip asked her what it was and she said hormones for her pre-menstrual syndrome. I suspect that she is an addict of some kind. It would explain the nonstop flashing teeth and the cruelty always so close to the surface.

She became nervous as my glance lingered too long on her face, laughed again, moved heavily to another of their relatives, saying, "Darling, it's been a coon's age!"

I have finally left David. Our son stayed with him last weekend and I attended the cocktail party celebrating the sixty-fifth birthday of Phillip's father. I helped Phillip choose the gift—a sweater I later realized the father would hate. I brought a bottle of Mumm's in a gray fabric bag with a grosgrain ribbon at the neck. Flowers, too, for Phillip's stepmother. They were barely acknowledged. One of the reasons I have always loved Phillip is because he has never said a word against his stepmother and yet I am certain he truly hates her. Naturally vicious myself, I admire his restraint.

My mind kept returning to David during the party, thinking that he would be home listening to jazz albums after putting Carlo to bed. Or perhaps he would have engaged our regular sitter and gone out on a date. The poor sitter—she always said we were the most beautiful couple and indeed we were.

Now, I have left David—no, rather, we have separated for good and I have moved out of our house because it was simpler that way— the house is old and big and I cannot fix the plumbing and I cry when mice and rats invade the basement. The sitter's father has left her mother for a girl who lives in Berkeley. She tells me exactly how much money he sends her mother and it is much more than David gives me for Carlo, though her father is only a security guard at Woolworth's.

David did not even want any of the photographs from our album. He said, "That's OK, you keep them," handing me twelve years of memories without flinching. Our courtship, the wedding photographs, the pictures of Carlo being born, the trip we took to Venice before David slept with the Chinese woman.

Phillip's family party soon became too much for me. His father and stepmother pretended they did not see me—they recognized my name—I was the married woman Phillip had been going out with for nearly a year. "Victoria"—the name alone sent their collective blood pressure zooming. Lenore was the only one who had met me before—she had said intimately, "Isn't he a hunk?" and then she showed me Phillip's baby pictures. Later, she talked behind my back, told Phillip I was using him.

It was a strange party. Phillip's father was cold and pedantic, wore lots of flashy jewelry, some of which he made himself. He sculpts lamps and necklaces. The stepmother, Nadine, is an Asian woman — Filipina, I guessed. The odd thing was that Phillip's brother Lewis was with his lover, George, also from the Philippines, who brought some sort of special treat to the party — garlicky, egg-rolley things I could not remember the name of. George's cousins and Nadine's children were there and I began to suspect that I was becoming paranoic, because ever since David slept with that woman when he was on a business trip in the Orient, I have felt inundated with Asians. Sometimes, when I talk with my sister on the telephone very late at night, I speak of "the yellow peril," knowing she will never quote me, that I need not worry about this indiscretion, this indulgence of my evil feelings.

Phillip's father's house unnerved me. It was furnished in motel-modern, with Asian decorator-accents, such as a furry tapestry of a tiger on the wall above the bar. I wondered what it had been like there before Phillip's mother died.

David once told me I was just like "Little Audrey" of the cartoons. Only a week after I moved out, Carlo and I saw a Little Audrey cartoon on television. She was bratty and gleeful with big eyes and wild hair like mine. I loved her and loved David and thought that I would write a cruel letter to the pastor who married us. He said he had never seen such an emotional couple at the altar. He gave me his handkerchief to cry into and I still have it.

Phillip's relatives do not think I am Little Audrey. They are a close-knit Jewish family, peppered with Asians, and think I am a strange, stiff little WASP who goes out with men while she is still married. They hope, clearly, that Phillip will get over it soon. They are wise enough to know that now that I am no longer David's wife, Phillip and I are not long for this world. Phillip always enjoyed drinking my husband's brandy more than any other brandy, and I noticed it and we all know it is the way Phillip is.

His older brother was condescending and supercilious. He pretended he did not catch my name. I knew that he knew and the entire family knew about "Victoria." The vixen, the shiksa, the white tornado. I resented Phillip's position in his family. Why could he not be a first-born as I am and as David is? We defer to no one in our families, while Phillip so readily accepts his pecking order. He looked up at Josh like a starlet at a producer, hung on his every word.

Phillip was fashionably dressed the night of the party, and in fact wore a necktie of David's I took with me when I moved — a pale leather tie from Italy. I knew Lenore was going to say, "Nice tie," touching it, and feared that Phillip might respond, "It's Victoria's husband's." In the car on the way over, I warned, "Just say it's from Italy."

Josh wore junk jewelry like the old man and towered over Phillip. His teeth were whiter, his hair was curlier, he was half a foot taller, his shoulders were much broader. Phillip looked like a cheap miniature of Josh, enjoying the position of Number Two.

Nadine, the stepmother, wore a tight sheath and looked quite lovely. Clearly she was years younger than the father and had undergone an expensive face-lift as well. I felt murderous.

I hyperventilated as I accepted a glass of punch from Phillip and took another of George's hors d'oeuvres. I knew it was neither Phillip's relatives nor anything else in the room that was making me breathe wrong — it was the thought of Woolworth's. Because when I thought of the babysitter's father being a security guard at Woolworth's, I remembered what happened three years ago, long before the sitter's father took up a gun there and left his wife for a girl. It was the time a pedophile snatched a boy Carlo's age from the Woolworth's candy counter and sodomized the child in a warehouse south of Market Street. The mother was choosing some nail polish on the crowded main floor and her son wandered three aisles away to admire the red and yellow Jujyfruits and the grape whips. The next thing she knew, the boy was gone. The following day, the child was released in the warehouse district, bruised and hysterical. He was so unhinged after being brutally raped for twelve hours that he forgot how to speak English, was babbling in Spanish to the police officers and sobbing. I read it all in the morning newspaper, sobbed and sobbed myself, would have begun raving in Spanish if I knew how. How can I defend Carlo and myself from the ugly and the rough, from those who steal and rape? Now, I live with Carlo only half the time, can protect him even less than before. What if David becomes engrossed in the hardware department and beautiful blond Carlo is snatched?

"Phillip, I don't feel well," I said, tugging at his sleeve.

"Your period?" he asked, sweet, ready to leave.

Your family, I thought. The world. The pedophiles and all the Suzy Wongs and everything I cannot understand and — worse — have no control over. Taking my husband, taking my child, wiping me off the map. But I told him, "I'm feeling rather 'fragile,'" and we said our goodbyes, Lenore adjourning to the bathroom when she saw us going for our coats. The father and Josh beamed arrogantly from behind their suntans and their glinting teeth. The teeth of the old man looked artificial, as did Josh's tan. Their jewelry glittered in the light as they waved goodbye.

I had to endure an eight-o'clock dental appointment the morning after the party. I sat in the chair hoping I would not offend the hygienist with my morning mouth. Claire performed her job well. She managed simultaneously to scrape and claw at my mouth and gums and to carry on a cheerful one-sided conversation. I offered the obligatory "Umm," and nodded my head at regular intervals. I was tired and felt weak after a restless night's sleep. About four times a week, I awaken in the middle of the night, very suddenly, and am unable to fall asleep again. I rise at dawn, see in the mirror that I am pale and have bags under my eyes, and after that I have diarrhea. "That's divorce, honey," said the secretary in my office when I confided to her.

"So, I'm taking a poetry course and a calligraphy class at the community college," Claire said. "I decided to combine them and write my poems in calligraphy."

I winced and hoped I could pass it off as a reaction to a rough jab to the gums.

"Last weekend, I wrote a poem and then did it in ink on a white fan," Claire told me, proud, and I nodded.

She asked me if I read "The Far Side" cartoon that morning in the newspaper, and when I shook my head, she went on to tell about a "dog-couple sitting at the breakfast table and . . ."

I began to sob in the brown leather chair. My head was pressed hard against the back of the chair and I felt as if I were ready to lift-off in the space shuttle.

Claire thought I had recognized the joke and was not sobbing but laughing, so she began to laugh along with me, enjoying sharing a laugh with one of the patients — until she saw, horrified, that the patient was crying.

I pulled my mouth away from her hands and from the instruments, mumbling, "I'm sorry, really sorry," and swallowed some mouthwash from the white pleated cup to my left, spit out blood and saliva and took the Kleenex Claire offered. I wiped away my tears and the liquid running from my nose.

"I feel like an idiot," I said. "I had no sleep last night."

Claire was kind and said, "Oh, lack of sleep can make a person very fragile," and put her hand on my shoulder. We both knew she meant: It is sad about you and David and of course you are crying.

The dentist, Dr. Shore, Dr. silver-haired rich Shore, came in to tell me I needed a filling replaced. He asked me casually if I still had dental insurance coverage. I have been his patient for fifteen years, and all the divorce means to Shore is that perhaps I will be dropped from David's policy and may not be able to pay my bill.

I left, humiliated, mascara running, lipstick tissued-off by Claire so that my lips were a bloodless white, and I knew they would all whisper that poor Vicky started crying in the chair — that the tears were falling on Claire's hand, that they would not stop.

It was possible to act tough, until the dentist's chair. I could quip and be cynical and droll about the divorce until I was lying back in a chair looking at the same dental office I have been going to since before I married David. Having someone's hand pulling back my lips and gums into a sardonic snarl, someone smelling my sour morning breath and watching the spittle drip from the corners of my mouth, digging at my mossy-feeling teeth and tender gums and poking until blood spattered my little bib—a baby's bib.

I knew I could never return to Dr. Shore's office. I must either let my teeth rot and fall out of my face, or find an anonymous dentist to clean them, or go to one of the franchise places where salesman-types clean teeth fast during the lunch hour in the office complexes in the financial district.

I decided I would let them rot. No one will probe me like that again, see my blood and tears and snot.

It seems I have more than my share of the theatrical events that sometimes occur in the normal course of daily life—things that seem too allegorical, too far out of the realm of natural possibility. For example, only a week before I found out about David's affair, a week before my life as I had known it for the previous nine years abruptly ended, I was interviewed downtown by one of the local radio stations' announcers—one of the "man-on-the-street" things. The question posed to me was this: "Are you lucky in love?" My exact answer is no longer part of my memory, but it was a definite yes, and I was apparently rather witty, as well. Several people I knew heard the interview when it was aired and spoke admiringly to me about it. The implausible truth is that David was actually in bed with another woman the very day I answered the question—the day I told the whole world— at least the greater Bay Area, that I was infinitely lucky in love, that Cupid was more or less my best friend.

Phillip, both superstitious and canny, always perceptive, telephoned me an hour after taking me home from his father's party. He had not spent the night with me because David was going to drop Carlo off at 6:30 in the morning so he could play golf before work.

"You're leaving me, aren't you baby—leaving me just like you left David," he said, voice calm but grave.

"I did not leave David," I corrected him, as if he did not know. "I simply moved out of the house because . . . "

"Aren't you? Leaving me?" he asked again, and I heard him strike a match and light one of his myriad, interminable cigarettes.

"No, of course not. Why?" I wanted to know. It was late and I had drunk much too much and was dizzily lying in the narrow space my body takes up now in the big bed, with only one-half of the dual-control electric blanket turned on. I was thinking, I will not need to leave you—you will leave me, now that I am free, but I said nothing.

"I *know*," he said. "And do you want to know how I know?" and I said that I would indeed like to know how he knew.

"Because my watch broke after I dropped you off," he said. If I did not know that Phillip has a particularly keen intellect, I might have begun to find him simple at that moment.

"You mean like, 'time's up'?" I asked, laughing loudly enough to cause an echo in the bedroom.

"The way you acted tonight at the party," he said, voice suddenly a trifle shrill. "You were so distant—you aren't the way you used to be. You want to drop me and find someone just like David, someone you think is more appropriate—someone who knows how to choose his own ties."

Oh my god, I thought. It is happening again. No one ever leaves me. They simply decide it is over with me and then proceed to make me so miserable, so tortured and hopeless and lonely that I have to go myself. Even my parents did it. Instead of asking me to move out when I finished school, they simply froze me out, treating me like the most unwelcome and distasteful boarder imaginable. I kept thinking it had to be a mistake of some sort—I was their *daughter*.

David could have left me. But if he had, he would have looked like the homewrecker, the abandoner. It was so much easier for him to have a casual sexual affair and let me find out about it. Then the onus was on me. I could either throw him out or let him stay so the wound would fester until the marriage was rotten, at which time he knew I would leave.

David shrugged when I found out about his fling — called it "irresistible," said it was "the most natural thing in the world — desiring someone, being curious." Later, when he discovered I had consoled myself with Phillip, he called me a "ruthless little whore."

"When I dropped you off at your house tonight," Phillip said next, "I banged my wrist on the car door as I pulled it shut. The watch stopped immediately. It still says 1:10, which is about one minute after you closed the door behind you."

"Very corny," I said.

We were both thinking and could practically hear each other thinking how odd it was that in fact I had given the wristwatch to Phillip, many months ago, after one of our first quarrels.

"Should I throw it out the window and see if time flies?" he asked.

I am going to miss Phillip a great deal. For I suspect his intuition was correct: I probably *will* leave him, just so he cannot leave me first.

I began searching for a funny old book I read when I was a little girl. It was old-fashioned even then. *A Girl of the Limberlost* it was titled, and I cannot even remember the author's name or if it is a serious work. A few nights ago, during one of my spells of insomnia, I remembered the book and ached to see it again. I could smell the musty old backing and see the worn brown cover — my parents had always had it among their motley selection of books — Reader's Digest condensed books and Booth Tarkington and Flaubert.

I can no longer remember the plot, except that it was about a very lonely girl who lived in a swamp with her aloof, unloving mother. The girl began catching butterflies in the marsh as a means of diverting her attention from the pain of her daily life. I remembered looking up "limberlost" in the family dictionary when I was about eleven years old, and the word was there. The other night when I thought of the book, I could no longer recall what the word means, so I got up in the middle of the night and looked it up in three dictionaries and it did not appear in any of them — not even the one from the book club that I have to lug out and read with a magnifying glass. The word has gone out of the language, at least for people who cannot afford three hundred dollars for a dictionary.

There are still some fine rare-book stores and tailors' shops in the "combat zone" of the city, the neighborhood with the porno shops and massage parlors and hamburger places, the places with signs on their fronts that read "Chinese Food and Donuts," where legless men ask for "spare change" and pimps jerk and twitch, say, "How ya' doing'?" leering. I decided one afternoon to brave the hookers and the street preachers in the defiled neighborhood and search out the book at Tandy's Antiquarian Books. I knew Tandy would watch for it if I told him how much I wanted to read it again.

I walked rapidly, with the studied posture and facial expression I learned in an anti-rape workshop, a demeanor that also discouraged beggars from approaching me. Out of the right side of my right eye, I saw doll faces in a window. They reminded me of the Kewpie dolls I used to see at the carnivals I went to with my grandparents out in the country when I was a little girl, so I stopped to look at them. As a girl, I loved the beautifully rouged and fluffy haired Kewpie dolls one could either win at the fair, or — desperate — purchase. I felt a quick surge of nostalgia as I looked at the row of them, but noticed they were disembodied. What were they? Just inflated doll heads, no bodies, painted faces, innocent staring eyes and open red lips.

David always told me that I tend to be somewhat stupid about the obvious, and I realize now that he was correct, because I stood admiring the Kewpie faces for some time before I finally realized that they had deep indentations beneath the scarlet lips on their faces. The sign on the store's facade said "Hot 'n Sassy," and I glimpsed a "battery-operated massager" in the lower segment of the window display.

I tried to imagine a man taking one of the synthetic heads into his bed and performing sexual acts on her latex face, but I could not.

The funniest, the worst, and the most grotesque and repulsive thing about the mouth dolls was that one of them was brown with black curls drawn on, one was golden haired and blue eyed, and one was a sallow color with eyes that slanted alluringly.

I decided I was becoming paranoic, after all, because it seemed as if they were placed in the window to arrest and disturb me as I came by chance past the shop, to make a wry comment on my life and times.

Am I "lucky in love?" Oh, yes — Cupid is practically my best friend — I have been arrow-shot.

I am sitting by myself at the kitchen table, watching my "boil-in-the-bag" frozen-dinner-for-one cooking. Carlo is with David and my apartment is cumbersomely silent. I catch a glimpse of my reflection in the toaster. It is a thirty-year-old Sunbeam I bought at a garage sale for four dollars, two weeks after I moved out of the house.

I see myself mirrored in the very center of the rounded facade of the toaster, small and solitary. Am I really so tiny, or is the rounded contour of the Sunbeam distorting my image? I look like a bumblebee — weeny little face and head, huge eyeglasses — or maybe a grasshopper, a locust. Motionless, small and ugly, in the middle of a toaster.

I realize for the first time that I will probably be by myself for the rest of my life. That I will hold onto Carlo for a few more years, be what every woman dreads — a "single parent." If I am fortunate, my son will not insist on living with David when he is old enough for such decisions. I will wake up alone in my bed year after year; I will try to be brave at Christmas time for Carlo's sake; I will carry in my own sacks of groceries forever.

I know, too, that if I cannot dissipate my bitterness, I am going to become as mean as Lenore, a tough cookie and a real racist and a man eater.

Phillip is right — time does fly, because it seems I have been sitting in my kitchen only a few minutes, but I smell an ugly chemical odor and realize that the water in the cooking pan has boiled away and the little plastic bag with my frozen casserole in it is beginning to melt down and burn up. It smells exactly as I remember Carlo's baby bottles smelling when I forgot about them and boiled them to nothing.

This time, I do not run to the stove with a potholder and grab the pan before it burns a hole in the bottom. This time, I sit in my chair and let the pan burn. I stare at the monstrous insect reflected in the toaster.

my higher power

In A.A., they tell you *never* to allow yourself to envy a person who is able to take a social drink. They tell you to simply accept that you yourself are not one of those persons, and that instead of pitying yourself and feeling jealous of those who can drink cocktails, you should just thank God that you have Alcoholics Anonymous and your sobriety. This never worked for me. I always felt a swift rush of self-pity when I watched people laughing over their beautiful glasses of champagne while I stood, stone-faced, with my Vichy water.

You can always take A.A.'s advice and slogans, however, and turn them around to suit another situation entirely. Fat people have taken "One Day at a Time" and used it to help them stay on their diets; depressed people have put bumper stickers on their cars, and they honk at each other in camaraderie on the freeway. So, when I see a happy couple somewhere, or — worse — a happy couple with their children, I tell myself never to allow myself to envy a happy couple. I remind myself that I am not part of a couple anymore, and I thank god I have a good divorce attorney.

When I am in the Home Improvement Center buying house plants and I see couples with their arms around each other picking out new floor tiles for the spacious kitchens in the homes they jointly own, see them hugging in the check-out line and looking as if they just won The Big Spin, I tense my abdominal muscles so that I do not feel my stomach as it flops over crazily in near nausea, and I dart my eyes about for a mirror or reflective surface so that I can see how nice I look that day, much more attractive than the woman of the happy couple. I try never to allow myself to think of the divorce in a negative or self-pitying frame of mind. In fact, I try to milk it for all it's worth. If a police officer pulls me over when I'm driving my car, I confess in a hushed voice, "I guess I wasn't paying attention, Officer. I'm being divorced," and I shrug sadly. Usually the cop lets me go.

Also, pleading "divorced" is a good way to avoid solicitation without looking like a tightwad. Like the time the chunky woman wearing Birkenstocks and a "PRIDE" button came to my apartment door to collect for the Women's Clinic. She told me in a combative tone, "This is the first time the Women's Clinic has had to solicit door-to-door. We've lost our funding." She glared at me as if unless I ponied-up she would assume I was on the men's side.

"*I've* lost my funding, too," I told her, and when I saw a look of shock and distaste cross her face, I cast my eyes down and said very softly, "My husband . . . I mean, I'm being divorced."

She turned the tables on me, though, that amazon with the clipboard. She said, "Oh, too bad," and thrust a sheaf of literature about the clinic at me. "You'll be needing our services, then," she said. "We're free."

I took the pamphlets, humiliated, and said nothing as she turned her back and bounded down the steps. I wanted to scream after her, "I don't need a free clinic! I have excellent medical insurance!"

Sometimes God—or what in A.A. they call "my higher power"—or even "H.P."—sends an Unhappy Couple my way, which is very helpful to me. Like when I was on the wagon and used to see loud drunks in restaurants, or lady winos with broken blood vessels on their faces and no stockings on their hairy legs and I would think, Phew, that could have been me, if I had not stopped drinking.

Now, all I need to make me feel fortunate is a couple like the one I saw yesterday near Union Square. They stood next to me at the crosswalk while we waited for the light to change, both of them lugging large suitcases. I could hear their labored breathing, see the sweat standing on their brows. I said cheerily to them, "You need a cab!" and smiled my broadest smile, the one I save for tourists and for the Salvation Army lady — the one who says, "Good morning, angel," to me every day and "God bless you," on the days I give a dollar.

The man of the unhappy couple gave me a look of sheer hate. His lips pulled back in a snarl and he said, "We're almost *there.*"

Shocked and hurt, I looked away. The woman said quietly to me, just as the light turned green, "I told him we needed a cab," and we exchanged a look.

When David and I separated, I used to go around saying to myself, "I wish I were dead; I wish I were *dead.*" Then I would feel guilty on Carlo's account — think how terrible it would be for Carlo to have a dead mother and to be brought up by robot-David and a terrible stepmother — whichever of David's young girlfriends he ends up marrying. But then, things grew worse. I stopped wishing I were dead and began wishing I were alive. I mumbled aloud in my apartment, "I wish I were alive. I wish I felt something." They say to be careful what you wish for — that you just might get it. Every time I wished I were alive, I would dream of Phillip and would be awakened by an orgasm so violent that I nearly fell out of bed, and then I would cry, because Phillip is in jail and has a lovely round ass and you know what that means.

When I wake up like that, too alive and wishing I were dead, I have to drink before work. It is usually about 4 A.M. when I have the earthquake while dreaming of Phillip, and I have to calm myself down with the vibrator after that. The vibrator is chicken-feed after dreaming of Phillip; it is like a calming drink of cognac. I spend the better part of an hour with it, thinking of Phillip, then not thinking of him, then talking dirty to myself for variety. I hope the people upstairs — a couple, naturally — do not hear me, but then I also think What the hell? It could be an electric razor, and let's face it, I don't really care what they think anyway. I have to smell their cooking all the time, coming through the heating ducts, the smell of garlic and contentment until I feel like going upstairs and punching them out. At times like this, I rise at 5 A.M. and drink two stiff vodka-cranberry juices and eat about a half-dozen whole-wheat fig bars, and I enjoy every second of it, even though I know the alarm will go off in forty-five minutes and that I will have to hop into the shower, take Carlo to school, and be in the office by eight o'clock, worrying about smelling of booze.

The last time I saw Phillip, I poured fifty-eight dollars worth of vodka and beer down the kitchen sink, though I badly needed a drink, and though I had only twelve dollars left in checking. That night, Phillip was the kind of drunk that he had begun to be in the previous months of our romance. He had always been a drunk, of course, but he had been an amorous or a funny or a carefree drunk. What he had become was a mean, boring, and rambunctious drunk, and the booze had become like super-fuel to him. I would drink, become silly, become sleepy, and then go to bed. Phillip would drink, become vicious, and then stay up. I would hear him crashing about the apartment until five or six in the morning, banging into things and swearing, laughing raucously in front of the television at 3 A.M. when the B-grade horror films were on, talking to himself while he went through the papers on my desk in the study.

Last time the trouble began in the Italian restaurant. He had been quiet but fairly pleasant, definitely on the subdued side that evening, but when the waiter brought the carbonara and the second liter of red wine, Phillip changed into the man I had begun to think of as "that other guy — the asshole."

I was telling him about the drugstore I had passed earlier in the day — that the window had been packed full of braces and canes and porta-toilets and that there had been a large sign advertising "Quad Canes — 20% off." I told him I had been horrified, imagining that "quad" referred to quadriplegics, but that I had then seen canes with four feet at the bottom featured in the window display. Suddenly Phillip put his utensils down hard on the table and looked at me with distaste. With a tough smirk he asked, "Did you know this dish had peas in it when you suggested ordering it?"

"What?" I said, stunned, feeling how far away I was from the quad-cane anecdote. I stared at the few green peas nestled rather prettily in the pasta I had recommended to Phillip.

I have known Phillip long enough to know that he detests peas, though as far as I can tell, he detests them for no other reason than that his father always liked them. I long ago learned never to order sizzling rice soup in a Chinese restaurant or that Phillip will first sulk and then pick out all the peas and put them in a pile in his rice bowl.

"No, Phillip," I responded, feeling immediately angry. "I didn't remember there were peas in it. I ordered it because you like pasta, though I don't, particularly." I used my fork like a dagger in the pile of noodles.

He looked at me as if to say, "Yeah, sure," and then looked out the window for a long time. He poured down two glasses of wine in less than two minutes and piled the peas high in an embarrassing, violently green pile.

He told me in a casual, offhand manner that he thought my best friend was nothing but a whore, and followed up by saying, "While I'm being honest, I also think you're a pretty poor mother to Carlo." He actually said "on-usht" like the drunks in cartoons do.

Maybe I lied when I said that Phillip is a mean drunk and I am not, because I felt a surge of rage when he said those things, but I did not show it. I smiled ingratiatingly and said, "Well, I'm sure I'll never be like your mother," and began rummaging in the pocket of my blazer so I did not have to watch his expression. Phillip knew perfectly well what I thought of his mother—an abusive manic-depressive who killed herself with drugs and booze.

You bastard, you bastard, you bastard, I thought. I discovered a strip of paper in my pocket and pulled it out. It was an old fortune from a fortune cookie. "Trust him, but keep your eyes open," it read.

I smiled and said, "Oh!" as if something extremely propitious had been foreseen for me, then I folded the fortune and put it into my purse so that Phillip would not see it. He was already paying the check and standing up.

Phillip would not leave after he drove me home, but pushed his way up the stairs and poured himself a tall vodka. I knew we were in for another long night. When he went into the bathroom, I poured every drop of alcohol in the house into the kitchen sink and brutally heaved the empty bottles into the garbage basket, enjoying breaking some of the beer bottles. I went to bed, and after he slammed out of the house I unplugged the telephone so he could not call me later when he was even drunker or had sobered up. I *never* want to see him again, I thought, as I yanked the phone cord from the outlet.

The police got him on Mission Street for drunk driving, driving with a revoked license, and a bench warrant for an accident he had been involved in a year ago.

He said later that my telephone rang one hundred and fifty times, but it never rang on my end at all.

I have a little rule of thumb I go by. It is this: Never drink unless you look good. What this means is that if I want to drink in the morning, for instance, as I sometimes feel like doing when Carlo is at David's and I wake up alone on Sunday morning, I do not allow myself to do it in my bathrobe. I get up, take a shower, mousse my hair, apply a little makeup, and slip into at the very least sweats, put on earrings. Then I tank up. This is the only way I have of gauging whether I have lost control or not. I know that if I start drinking in my robe before my shower, I will have lost it. I know that I will then be a grotesque bum of a woman when I pass out, instead of a sad lady "falling asleep." Besides, sometimes I run out of booze and have to go down to the Safeway for more.

Saturday, in fact. I had planned to shop for new sheets and towels at a white sale, but I had a Bloody Mary first, and began writing a letter to Phillip, and the next thing I knew it was twilight and the vodka was gone. I put on my sunglasses, freshened my lipstick, and walked to the Safeway. There was a young man in the parking lot, and I do not know whether he was really a Jesus-freak or just pretending to be, but as we passed each other, he stared at my breasts and sang, "Oh, praise the Lord! Praise God's name."

Furious, I never looked his way, but as I walked past him, I made a face as if I were vomiting.

"Jesus loves you!" he shouted in retaliation.

"Well, he doesn't love *you!*" I told him.

Not long before the night they took Phillip away, I began to think of the streetlight outside the front window of my flat as God. I would look directly into its glaring half-dome when I drank on the sofa in the dark. In the distance behind it I could see the red and yellow clam-shell sign of the all-night gas station I used to go to before they made me surrender my credit card. Usually I would go to the streetlight after I awoke around 2:30, my heart beating fast while I felt my way to Carlo's room to see if he was still there. If he was, I leaned over his bed and listened to his sweet breathing. His bed is just like mine; David built them for us when I moved out of the house. David kept our king-sized bed, and Carlo's bed had been built into the wall, so that when we moved, we had no beds to take. Two weeks before I moved out, I refinished the old bureau that had been mine as a child, but that David and I had shared for more than a decade. While I sanded, David sawed and hammered, making beds for Carlo and me. I noticed that he used cheaper wood and thinner foam than he had used for our king-sized bed, but I was grateful anyway.

If Carlo is not in his Dad-made bed when I go to his room at these times, I remember he is at David's and I resign myself to the fact that I am entirely alone and that Carlo and I are both fortunate that David and I have joint custody. In either case, I pour myself a deep vodka, because I know I have to go to work at eight o'clock and that I will not fall back asleep without alcohol. I sit on the sofa in the dark and quiet of the night, drinking myself to sleep, and I look at the streetlight which ruins my beautiful view and yet makes me feel safe when I come home late. I cannot imagine being mugged in such a bright light, and it is positioned exactly in front of the house. After the second vodka, I fix my eyes on the streetlight and resume the prayers that I ceased at age sixteen after I found out they were never answered. "Dear God," I say, eyes fixed on the light, a Job's Daughter again, dewy-eyed supplicant to the Father and the Son, "Dear God, I need someone to love. Not Phillip, please, but someone normal — someone who *wants* love." I stare into the light, unblinking, for a long time, wishing, but He sends Phillip every time — it is the damnedest thing.

I woke up with hives this morning. I have not broken out since last Christmas, when David and I spent the day together for Carlo's sake and I came out in hives after dinner from the strain of not screaming. David had tacked photographs of his twenty-three-year-old Chinese girlfriend all over the kitchen wall, and I was forced to pretend I did not see them. There was Chinese script on the chalkboard where I used to write the grocery list, and David actually ate his turkey stuffing with chopsticks. I could not whip him with my napkin or strangle him, because I did not want to ruin Carlo's Christmas, and also because David gave me several large bills in a Gucci wallet for Christmas and how can you choke someone when he does that?

Today I took some of the antihistamines Dr. Walker prescribed for me at Christmas, rubbed some cortisone cream on the bumps, and poured a little cognac into my morning coffee to cheer myself up. Whenever my son goes to camp, I get a little crazy, which is probably what made me go over to the house last night. Carlo called me yesterday afternoon from Camp White Cloud; they encourage the kids to call home when they feel like it.

"Hello, may I speak to Victoria, please?" he said, and I responded, "For godsake Carlo, I'm the only one here!" Clearly he is going to be exactly like David when he grows up, unable to lighten up enough to say, "Hi, Mom." It is probably for the best, however, as I would not want him to grow up to be like me. I choked back tears as we finished talking, saying, "See you Saturday, honey," and feeling as if I would never see him again.

There was a postcard from Santa Rita from Phillip, and even after reading it five times, I could not decide whether it was one of his jokes or if he was trying to run some kind of a scam in jail. It was a regular U.S. Postal Service card, and said, "Dearest Victoria, I am urging you to go back to A.A., as I have been attending meetings here, have decided not to resume drinking when I am released, and know my entire life has changed because of this decision. I wish the same for you, sweetpea. Also, I have accepted Jesus Christ as my personal saviour. Aren't you surprised, babe? Love, Phillip."

If there is one person in this world who will never give up booze and who would rather die than accept Christ, it is Phillip Shapiro. Though not staunchly or orthodoxly Jewish, he has always had a healthy distaste for Jesus and finds all Christian traditions to be vulgar and honky-tonk. I cannot decide if his sense of humor has become even more twisted than ever after nearly two months of being deprived of booze and sex-as-we-knew-it, or if he is trying to pull one of those "born again" numbers so he can try for an early release.

I began to feel blue, though, after I finished laughing at the card. I thought of Carlo in his little bunk at camp with a lot of children I do not even know; David living with our dog in our house, which is for sale and which has Chinese writing on the chalkboard now; Phillip in jail pretending to be a Christian and maybe having to do things with men. I drank quite a bit while I composed letters to Carlo and Phillip, and then I broke my rule about not driving the car when I am potted. I drove, rather than walked to the Safeway, and none too steadily. Except that I passed the Safeway and went to the house. I did not know I was going to go there, but I headed straight for the house, feeling like I felt when I was twelve and ran away from home, except the farthest I ran was to the back seat of my father's car, where I hid, crouched on the floor and weeping until midnight.

There is a tacky red and white "For Sale" sign in front of our house, and a lockbox over the door so realtors can traipse in and out all day with people who want to live in the house where David and I were once happy. I let myself in — David knew better than to ask me to give back my key, and often Carlo and I go over there anyway to pick up toys or clothes. I heard Misty, our golden retriever, crying when I entered the house, but it was muffled crying, coming from the bathroom. I flung the bathroom door open to find Misty wagging her tail with a miserable expression on her face, desperately happy to see me. Some slimeball realtor had locked my dog in the bathroom.

I erased the foreign writing from the board, poured myself some of David's brandy and went upstairs with Misty to lie on my old bed and weep. "Misty, oh Misty, oh, girl-pup, my dearest pup," I cried, a rummy crying jag, crying myself to sleep there, just as I did when the whole thing fell apart for David and me.

It was dark when I awoke, and I had a bad case of the spins. At first, I could not remember where I was. And then I knew it was our old bed and recalled that I had let myself into the house where I no longer live. They were talking in the living room, but I could not hear what they were saying.

"David?" I called out, my voice quavering. "It's Vicky . . . I'm sorry, but I'm here." I heard the girlfriend scurry into the den. Smart girl, I thought. Maybe she will not be such a bad stepmother to Carlo after all, if she knows enough to run when she hears me coming.

David was clown-white when he came to the top of the stairs, and I could see that he was both concerned and still afraid of my bad temper.

"What's wrong?" he asked. "What are you doing here? Are you all right?"

"It's our girl," I cried. "Some fool locked up our girl," and I wept into David's arms, just the way I used to. When I saw the shadow moving on the hallway wall, I closed my eyes.

microslips

When my lover had been dead for eight weeks, I realized I needed to get the dog back from my ex-husband. Fifty-six days of sleeping alone in my bed was getting to me. There would be another 309 such nights before even the first year without Phillip was over. It was highly likely that these hundreds of nights would turn into thousands.

David never let Misty sleep with us when we were married — his idea of comfort did not include a large, hairy golden retriever in bed between him and his wife. Usually, Misty had slept in our son Carlo's bed, but when our marriage began to fall apart, when David went off to live on a houseboat, when he stated that "marriage is too confining," I let Misty sleep with me, her furry head on David's pillow. She would go to bed with Carlo at nine o'clock, then join me later when I went to bed. Sometimes I would wake in the middle of the night to find her pinning my shoulders down with her paws and staring at my face like a lover. When I opened my eyes, she would begin licking me furiously.

There are billions of people in the world, and hardly any of them sleep in bed alone. In the United States, many children sleep alone, though this is not always true in other countries. In some countries, entire families share a bed. In much of the world, couples sleep together every night from shortly after adolescence until death. Of all the billions, it is only a sad, twisted few adults who sleep alone all night in a bed. The thought of the hundreds, thousands of nights ahead of me with no sound of breathing in my bed made me feel sick.

During the divorce proceedings, I told my lawyer firmly, "I want joint custody of the golden retriever." My lawyer looked at me with an expression of mingled amusement and pity and said, "Let's just call the dog Carlo's and let it all work out around that, OK?" Shamed, I dropped the subject.

And the truth is I had no place to keep Misty. The lease barred pets of any kind, so I'd had to sneak Misty into the building the few times she came to stay with Carlo and me when David was out of town on business. It did not work out all that well having her in my flat. Misty had been house-broken to use a doggie-door — I trained her myself when she was only seven weeks old; she was a Christmas present for Carlo. She was used to scooting out the hinged square in the door and relieving herself anytime she felt the need. When she stayed with us in our flat on Palm Avenue, she awakened me twice during the night, shaking my shoulder and running in frenzied little circles that told me she had to go outside. I did not love any animal quite enough to walk it twice in the middle of the night, so Misty became solely David's after that.

But things would have to change. Perhaps Carlo and I would have to move to a rented house with a yard, so I could get Misty back and let her sleep in my bed again. I would much rather sleep with a dog's muzzle next to my face than a blank pillow that smells slightly of bleach.

I asked Phillip's former psychiatrist what things would be like for me now. I asked Dr. Roth how I was to make it through my first year of grief, and what I was to expect. I wanted to know how long I would continue to hear what sounded like car horns blowing loudly in my ears. The day Phillip died, I thought I heard a wedding procession driving by, car horns blaring as the wedding party moved from the church to the reception in their automobiles. The next morning, I awoke from a few minutes sleep to hear the horns again. So early in the morning for a wedding, I thought, and on a weekday. "It must be a Filipino wedding," I said to Carlo.

He looked at me with a strange expression and asked, "What do you mean, Mom?"

I didn't know. "I don't know," I told him. "It just *must* be."

The car horns were like the bright light that washed my life in a blinding glare now. Phillip left, they arrived; Phillip did not come back, they did not leave.

"The noise and the light are part of the shock," Roth said. "That will pass within days, I imagine." He paused, then went on matter-of-factly. "At the three-month mark, you'll begin to feel much better. In fact, at times you'll be euphoric."

I laughed loudly, laughed in Roth's face. Euphoric? In the wake of Phillip's death? "No," I told Roth, but he ignored me.

"Then after that, I warn you, at six months it gets somehow worse."

I snorted, shaking my head, no. "It couldn't *be* any worse," I said.

"Yes, it does get worse," he told me, radiating absolute certainty. "You'll first be euphoric, you will then begin to get used to the idea that Phillip is dead and you will feel a bit numb. Then at six months, you'll fall into a pit of despair."

I relished the idea of falling into any pit and being able to stay there. I visualized myself tripping on some precipice — maybe one just like the one I'd nearly fallen off at the beach with Roth the day Phillip's ashes were thrown out of a rented airplane — falling deep into the pit and disappearing forever.

Roth said sadly, "Just when you start to think you might be getting over it, it will really hit home, Victoria. You'll realize that half a year has gone by, you have somehow survived, but that you will never, ever see Phillip again, and it will be horrible, because you won't have the benefit of shock as a buffer at that point. You will experience it rationally and fully."

I did not believe him. There would be no euphoria, there would be no despair any worse than what I already felt. He started telling me about what happened to him after his father died, and relating stories to me about bereaved patients, but I did not listen. I just stared at Roth, wondering how he could face me after handing me a bag full of

Phillip's belongings, telling me Phillip had left them there in the office for me. I guessed that when the shock did wear off, I might report him to the Medical Society as a charlatan and a menace. But who would believe me? I was what the newspapers would term "a former mental patient."

And the awful truth was that I loved Roth, in a way. My only desire other than to die and be with Phillip, was to be cradled in Roth's arms, rocked like a baby, kissed tenderly on the back of my neck, to hear Roth say, "It's all right, Victoria — it's all right."

"I don't want to fall for you," I told him, the last time I saw him in his office. I told him I was terminating therapy. He responded by asking me to lunch. "I'll have lunch with you, maybe dinner, but I won't fall for you," I said.

"We can be friends, real friends," the treacherous psychiatrist told me. He hugged me to his body, speaking of friendship, and I could smell the warm perspiration resulting from his lust. He spoke of being my friend — the man who handed me a five-hundred-dollar I.O.U. Phillip had made to a friend, and claimed I had dropped it in his office. It was all right — I paid Phillip's friend the money. I knew Phillip asked Roth to see that I paid off the loan, so I did. But I knew the I.O.U. had not fallen out of my purse or the box full of papers I carried around — I knew Roth planted it so he would never have to admit to me that he and Phillip sat down together and planned Phillip's suicide. I knew Roth had done nothing to intervene.

"I think I may have fallen for *you* already, though," Roth said and provided comic relief by pretending to trip. "Whoa!" he cried, tripping on the oriental rug and paddling the air with his arms as he pretended to take a header.

All I could think of, barely acknowledging Roth's fake pratfall, was Phillip's falling-down job. Phillip had failed to show up for one of his Vegas stage magic gigs, and had shown up drunk for a minor gig at a birthday party in Hillsborough, and he was briefly blacklisted. There was a period of a few months when he had no magician's work at all and lost thousands gambling as well. Desperate for rent money, he answered a newspaper ad that posed the question, "Will you be a fall guy for Science?" Phillip learned he could earn twenty dollars an hour on a temporary basis as a participant in a local university's industrial engineering department, which was doing a study of slipping and falling. The scientist in charge of the project told Phillip that four thousand Americans die in falls every year, and yet no one has any idea why or how people fall. "You know it's a slip," the man told him, "but you don't know why."

For a few hours a day Phillip wore a harness connected to a revolving mechanical arm. He had reflective Ping-Pong balls taped to his shoulder, elbow, wrist, hip, knee, ankle, and foot. He walked in circles for two hours at a time, filmed by video cameras, repeatedly crossing about fifteen feet of slick steel plate placed in front of the cameras. Whenever he slipped, the cameras recorded where the Ping-Pong balls were in space.

The study found that Phillip slipped forward, then jerked sideways as a physical reaction, but it was not known what this indicated. Phillip told me that the experiment had also discovered that everyone has what is known as "microslips," that every time one puts his foot on the ground, there is a slight slip — up to a centimeter — but that usually one does not perceive it. The study was trying to find out just exactly when it is that a person begins to perceive a slip — when one realizes that he is indeed falling, rather than going on, completely unaware of having slipped and almost fallen to the ground.

"You shouldn't go to lunch with Dr. Roth," Carlo told me.

"Why not?" I asked, surprised.

"It's his fault," he said calmly, stuffing books and sporting equipment into his backpack before I drove him to school the day I was to meet Roth at Stars for lunch.

"It?" I asked, blank for a moment. "You mean what happened to Phillip?"

"Yes, it's his fault," Carlo repeated.

I was surprised that Carlo would bring up the matter. He was still angry about Phillip damaging his mother, abandoning us both. He cried only one time — two weeks after Phillip's death — when he was playing Nintendo by himself in the living room. Carlo had turned off the television and walked briskly down the hall with tears glistening in his eyes. "What is it?" I cried.

"That was the same game Phillip and I were playing the last time we ever had fun together," Carlo said, but wriggled away when I tried to hug him. He never mentioned Phillip again, except to tell me coldly that David said Phillip was "crazy and no good."

I knew David had not planted the idea in Carlo's head, however, that Dr. Roth was responsible for Phillip's death. He would have had no way of knowing anything about Roth except what I told him about the funeral the two of us held alone at the beach.

"Dr. Roth was Phillip's psychiatrist," Carlo said. "It was his job to save Phillip's life. He didn't do it. Who else would you blame?" He turned his back to me and began rummaging for pencils in his desk drawer.

"Myself, maybe," I said in a squeaky little voice, "Or . . . just the gambling problem — he was always humiliating himself."

"Roth's a bad doctor," Carlo told me, training his clear blue eyes on me — he looked exactly like David, except he had my freckles on his face and my full bottom lip. "If he was a good doctor, he'd have helped Phillip and he'd be alive."

"Were," I said.

"What?" Carlo asked.

"If he *were* a good doctor, not if he *was.*"

Carlo was not thrown off track. "Phillip was paying him lots of money to help him, and look what happened. I don't know why you want to eat lunch with him."

I drove Carlo to school, went to the office and pretended to work for three hours, and at twelve o'clock I went to Stars to meet Roth. My son says it's your fault, I would tell Roth when he arrived. Children know these things, I would say. You planted the I.O.U.; you had all of Phillip's favorite belongings — you had the nerve to hand them to me the day he died as if they'd dropped from the sky. You had him all doped-up and crazy — I happen to know you even gave him a book on rational suicide from the Hemlock Society.

I told the maitre d' that I would wait for Roth at the bar, and I went in and ordered a martini. I was surprised Roth kept me waiting for even five minutes — he had always been prompt for our appointments and had once come into the office wearing a woolen muffler around his throat and croaking with bronchitis to see Phillip and me for couples' counseling. "You two I cannot miss," he said, but he looked straight at me as he said it, which Phillip either failed to notice or did not mention.

The waiter came up to me with a cordless telephone. "Miss Wright?" he said in a hushed tone, "Dr. Roth is calling — an emergency."

Oh, Christ, I thought, but I was titillated by taking my very first phone call in a restaurant. "What is it Paul?" I asked.

"I'm doing a deposition, Love," he told me, and I wondered if he were being sued. "We were supposed to be finished before twelve." He laughed strangely. "I've had to go off-record here so this won't appear in the transcript." I realized he was sitting in a room with a gaggle of lawyers who were listening to every word he said. "Can you wait half an hour — will that work out? You could order an appetizer — do you have a book with you?"

"Of course," I answered.

What was it about Roth's sense of timing? Had he shown up on time or ten minutes late, I probably would have been cold or sulky, then launched into a tirade about his being responsible for Phillip's death. Instead, he was making me wait alone for half an hour, and I knew I was intrigued by his absence and his "deposition" and that when he arrived, I would be smiling, happy, mollified by a cocktail and an appetizer and curious about why he was late.

I told the waiter I would like to be seated and have an appetizer before my companion arrived. I said we would prefer to eat in the room with the bar and the piano, that the elevated room with the mirrors was too bright for us. I like watching the people at the bar and wanted to avoid sitting next to gabby socialites in the supposedly preferable section of the restaurant, seeing myself reflected in the wall mirrors, rereading Celine at my table. The waiter was a shaved-headed black man with one gold hoop earring, who seemed angry with me and called me "Madame" in a mean voice. I was not sure if he was mad because I wanted to be seated before "the rest of my party" arrived, or if he did not approve of my reading at table, or if he just hated women. He was very solidly built and the kohl eyeliner he wore was barely visible.

I tend to border on the anorexic and had no desire to order anything to eat before Roth arrived. But I had read an article in a men's magazine at the hairdresser's that complained that men are extremely turned off by women who will not eat, or who order wispy little salads and pick at them, which would have been my inclination. I remembered that Roth talked about food a lot, so I decided I would try to eat heartily that day. I ordered carpaccio so he would know I had a taste for blood. I won't say that the waiter slammed it down upon the table, but the china did clink as he placed it before me.

"He's a bit of a bastard," I said, raising my cheek to be kissed. Roth kissed my ear, either a hit or a miss, and dropped into his chair, waving desperately at the waiter to return, and mouthing, "Stoli up!" to Mr. Clean.

"Are you being sued?" I asked, watching Roth stare hard at the raw beef and capers.

"No, no," he said, heaping thin slices of meat onto his bread plate. "May I have a sip of your martini to tide me over until Baldy brings me my drink?" he asked. "I'm a wreck."

He took a drink and then said he was simply a witness for a probate matter of some sort. "The guy wasn't even a patient of mine," Roth said, handing the martini back to me. "I saw him once and referred him to someone else — it's just that I was the last doctor to see him before he died."

My wrist spasmed and the cocktail flew up out of the glass and into Roth's face. "Why did you do that?" Roth said, wild eyed, wiping off his face and grabbing a napkin to blot up the large wet spot on the front of his shirt.

"I'm so sorry, Paul," I said, mortified. "When you said 'died,' I twitched." I turned to look for the waiter, who was approaching our table with Roth's vodka in his hand. He laughed aloud.

"A direct hit—congratulations, Miss," Mr. Clean said to me, admiration transforming his face. "Allow me to get you another."

"It was an accident!" I protested, and the waiter's laughter trilled out into the room.

"I'm sorry Victoria," Roth said. "I keep forgetting how on the edge you still are . . . that it's really only been a few weeks since . . . "

I cut him off, pointing to the two empty stools at the end of the bar. "That's where Phillip and I sat the last time we were here," I said. "We had a huge fight as usual."

"He was flirting with someone?" Roth asked. He drank deeply of his Stoli and closed his eyes luxuriously. He flushed attractively as he drank—not the usual florid shimmer of an alcoholic, but a sensual, healthy-looking blush.

"No," I said. "For once the fight wasn't over a woman. It was because he chatted up a Satanist at the bar and dragged me over to meet him."

"A Satanist? What do you mean?" he asked, staring at my breasts.

"You know that guy Victor Bileau, the local media hero of the Satanist cult? He was big a few years ago—they were always trying to bust him for something. He kept a black panther in his house as a pet and held lewd rituals there with sex on the altar, et cetera." Roth said that he vaguely remembered something of the kind. "I saw him sitting at the bar with a bleached-blond girl who looked nearly young enough to be his granddaughter. She had on little black lace gloves with no fingers in them, and she sat listening to him talk, never saying a word herself. I pointed them out to Phillip, said, 'Look, there's the Satanist, Victor Bileau, in the flesh.'"

Paul Roth was alternating between scanning the menu and giving me lascivious glances—he was not an attentive listener. Roth and I were both big talkers and often fought for the floor. "And then?" he asked.

"Well, Phillip's face just lit right up and he watched the couple really closely as they moved from the bar to a table. 'He *looks* satanic!' Phillip said, all rapt. I commented that anyone who wears a little pointed goatee and has a fixed stare as if on dope could manage to look sinister."

"Are you folks ready to order?" the waiter asked, his hand on the back of my chair. After tossing the drink into Roth's face, I had worked my way onto the waiter's "A" list. I asked Roth to order for us, and watched him carefully as he ordered pasta and fish and little baby this and little baby that and some sort of leek dish. He was dressed in extremely expensive Marin County rich hippie clothes, his silk shirt open vulgarly in front. He had the nerve to wear barefoot sandals in Stars. But he did these things somehow innocently, so childishly that it was touching. He reminded me of an adolescent in the first pathetic attempts to dress like a grown-up—the way Carlo might look in a couple of years. I remembered myself at thirteen, putting on crimson lipstick and my mother's high heels to have dinner at a hotel in the City with my friend's family on her birthday. The mother had laughed gaily and said, "Oh, Vicky!" I had been baffled by her response.

"Go on . . . what about Victor the Devil?" Roth asked, taking my hand and kissing my fingertips in a way he never would have done in his office. This was the first time we had ever been together without my insurance covering the hour as a medical expense. This time Roth would pay the bill.

"Well, Phillip excused himself to go to the men's room a few minutes later," I said, "and he was gone a really long time. Finally I started to look for him, thinking he was probably nuzzling up to some old girlfriend he'd run into, but instead I saw him in animated conversation with Bileau! Their faces were only inches from each other and they were laughing and talking like friends for life. He'd just sneaked off and chatted up the Satanist and his girlfriend, leaving me at the bar like a patsy. I went to the pay phone and called a taxi."

"Did you just leave him there and take off?"

"No, Phillip spied me at the phone, grabbed the telephone and canceled the cab, and literally dragged me to Bileau's table. I was furious — in a rage. 'Victor saw you at the bar — he asked to meet you,' Phillip said, and presented me to Bileau like some sort of female sacrifice."

"You do embellish, my dear," Roth said, slugging back his second vodka.

"Paul, you should learn to like mixed drinks," I said. "You shouldn't drink booze straight like that." He laughed at my hypocrisy. I had switched to white wine after one martini.

I gave up on telling the anecdote; clearly Roth had lost interest in the story and wanted to alternately eat and hold hands. We began eating the leeks and smiling dreamily at each other, but I thought about the rest of the story.

As soon as Bileau had looked up and fixed his hypnotic stare on my face, I stopped struggling in Phillip's grip and acted as if I were in a formal receiving line. "Very pleased to meet you," I said, shaking Bileau's chilly hand. "How do you do?" and "Charmed, my dear," to the little blond girl he called "Minx."

"Phil tells me you know of me?" Bileau said.

"Of course, darling — my name is Vic, too," I answered, the consummate phony. I excused myself and stood smoldering at the cab stand, hating Phillip's guts. "Why are you so perverse?" I hissed when he came to drag me away from the taxi. "Why do you find trouble and filth and just suck right up to it every time?"

He laughed aloud and we began to tussle a bit. The tussling and slapping led into some steamy kissing and then we both began laughing, and that was the end of our adventure with the Satanists.

"That guy Victor Bileau?" Roth said suddenly. "I remember now — his real name's Victor Blume. He's Jewish. His father's a rabbi."

I laughed a high-pitched laugh, astonished, and when Roth saw the silly look on my face he burst into hysterical laughter like a little kid, spitting a huge mouthful of vodka into my face in the process. I laughed breathlessly and shook the liquid from my eyeglasses.

"We see the gentleman's getting even," the waiter said.

I never believed much in prayer. Like many kids, I used to beg God for the things I wanted, but I seldom got them. One only believes in magic if the illusion is fulfilled. While still preadolescent, I decided that since prayer did not seem to yield results, I was going to give it up. The begging was unappealing enough to me even when God came through, but the fact was He usually ignored my requests anyway, so that the act of pleading was insult added to injury.

One's own rules become less rigid, however, as one grows older. I resumed prayer in my thirties — the plan being that I would never ask for something for myself, but would pray only for the welfare of others. I prayed for baby Carlo all the time, beginning shortly after his birth; but I suppose that was cheating, since I certainly had a vested interest in his health and welfare. If the pope appeared on television and asked everyone to pray for peace, I did so. I prayed as well for the parents of my friends when the old folks had strokes or heart attacks and their lives hung in the balance.

Who actually drove me to my knees, though, was Phillip Shapiro. Four years before his death, he announced sadly to me that he was taking his life. He stopped vacuuming his house, so that dust devils flew around us as we made love. He boxed-up all my letters in one of his theatrical trunks, padlocked it, and taped a label on it addressed to me. He stopped eating and became spacey and ethereal, subsisting on brandy and vitamin C caplets. He must have eaten something more, but I didn't see him do so and he became very thin. I was horribly concerned, frantic, and telephoned both Lewis and Lenore to express my fears for their brother. Lewis lisped that Phillip had been "doing this regularly since his live-in girlfriend left him," and slammed the telephone receiver down in my ear. I was put in my place, I suppose: Phillip wanted to die because of the woman before me, I was being told. Even from his despair, Phillip managed a chuckle when I told him about it. We exchanged a brief comradely glance before his eyes glazed over again.

Lenore laughed when I called her. She told me Phillip had been threatening suicide for years—that it was a ploy to get the family to pay his rent. "You'll notice that these events always take place near the first of the month," she chortled, laughing her sonorous fat-lady's laugh.

Phillip telephoned me on Friday night and said, "I love you Victoria—it's not your fault," and hung up mysteriously. When I called him back, there was no answer. It was my opinion that if he had really planned to die, he would not have made such a theatrical telephone call. I had to go with Lenore on this one and assume Phillip simply wanted me to urge the family to pay his rent.

I had overdosed on interaction with Lewis and Lenore and decided to sit this one out. David was home three days in a row for the Labor Day holiday weekend, so there was no way I could get away and drive across the Bay to check up on Phillip. I crept upstairs to the princess phone and called Phillip's number every chance I had, but the phone just rang and rang.

I visualized him sitting in the rose-colored armchair, smoking cigarettes and smirking every time the telephone rang, just waiting for Lenore to panic and cough up the rent. Or maybe he thought I would pay it? That I would steal money from Carlo's college fund and give it to my lover?

I visualized him crying, hating himself for being a broken-down gambler and stage magician, unable to stop his downward spiral—barely able to recall that only a few years before he had been a Harvard grad on his way up. I pictured him laying his beautiful head down on the pillow we so often shared, swallowing a whole bottle of anti-depressants and having a seizure, aspirating on his vomit.

Every time David went into the bathroom, or out into the garden with Carlo, or to the driveway to squirt his car or a rose bush with the hose, I would drop to my knees with a thud. "Please, God, please spare Phillip," I begged, with my eyes squeezed shut and my hands clasped dramatically in front of me in the air. Even as I prayed, I felt unreal, felt as if I were still in my angel costume for the kindergarten Christmas pageant, my gold-trimmed wings glistening thrillingly. Or like a Job's Daughter in my teens, kneeling in the white satin robe with the purple cord beneath my bosom, my hands clasped in prayer, the way they were now as I prayed for Phillip. "Nearer, my God to Thee," the daughters of Job sang together, by candlelight, kneeling in the shape of a cross, tears shining in their eyes, hormones raging. "Please, God, don't let Phillip die," I begged, shaking my head to get rid of the Job's Daughter image and trying to pray in a serious manner, not wanting God to see me as doing some sort of Hollywood prayer.

"Phillip is good and sweet, Lord," I said. "He's weak and half-crazy, but he's one of your dearest children — please don't let him kill himself." I tried to bargain with Him: "God, I ask nothing for myself. If necessary, I'll never even see Phillip again. But spare his life, and I'll love him and love him and love him and he'll find his way — love will make him flourish," I promised.

I believe God heard me. I went to Phillip's door that Tuesday morning before work after not hearing his voice for three days and three long nights. He opened the door to me passively, pale and with a swollen face and blackish eyelids, his hair matted down like a crazy hair-hat. "What happened?" I gasped.

"I took all my pills and lived," he said matter of factly, gesturing for me to come in and sit down. He was smoking, and I wondered how he always had money for cigarettes, even when he had none for rent or food or even brandy.

He had bruises all over his arms and on one side of his face. "I just woke up a few hours ago," he said. "I've been sleeping since Friday night when I took thirty of my pills." He looked down at himself and smiled. "I seem to be all beat up, though," he said. "It's curious."

I never really figured out what happened that weekend. My friend Sheila always teased me about it, telling me Phillip was a real con man. "He took six aspirin and unplugged the phone," she quipped, saying it was like one of the fake suicide tries convicted felons stage to garner sympathy before being sentenced.

Part of me agreed with Sheila. The rest of me believed that Phillip took the thirty antidepressant tablets and lay down to die and that God heard me beg for the life of my lover, my best friend.

Four years later, I did not pray. Phillip saw to that. By invoking the name of an old girlfriend before he walked out of my house for the last time, he knew he gained at least four days of solitude, all the time he needed to make his exit without fear of discovery. There was nothing else that could have kept me from Phillip's door, could have made me refrain from calling an ambulance, could have guaranteed that I would not call Dr. Roth, would not go to Phillip's house and break the bedroom window myself if he failed to answer the door.

"I borrowed money from Paulette Beard." Those words were Phillip's ticket to oblivion, all right. When I first met him, he sometimes wore a button on his lapel that said "BeLIEve," and at first glance, one saw only the word "believe" and not the "LIE."

There was no wear and tear on my knees the day before Phillip died. Rather than praying for his bittersweet life, his little speck of terra firma, I was busy writing hate-letters to Phillip. Friends claim I'm being self-important to think this, but I know full well I kicked my lord-on-earth straight into the crematorium with my pointed-toe, high-heeled shoes.

I considered it — thought about praying for Phillip's life, the morning Dr. Roth telephoned me at my office and asked me innocently as a child, "When was the last time you saw Phillip?"

"Sunday night," I answered, wondering why he wanted to know. What did it matter if it had been two days or two weeks or two months, he always came back, or I went to him; it would always be so.

"Oh-oh," Roth said. He sounded exactly like Carlo used to sound when he was about two years old. When a mother hears her small child say, "Oh-oh," she runs full-speed toward the child with a sponge-mop and a broom and a can of Band-Aids.

"What? WHAT!" I demanded of Roth, feeling panic, and closing my eyes to recall Phillip's handsome straight spine walking away from me Sunday night — seeing him flinch as I threw his jacket onto his head from the upstairs window and blinded him momentarily. He never looked back, just picked up the jacket and walked away.

"He didn't show up for his appointment this morning. He's never done that before," Roth said. "He's not answering the phone."

I was physically electrified, lighted up. I had not felt such a sensation since the time Phillip and I took Ecstasy and it hit us in the car like a bolt of lightning. "Please, God, let him be all right," I started to say, but I bit the words off before they hit my tongue. It's too late, I thought — don't break your heart. I knew it was Kierkegaardian — it was an either/or situation. Either Phillip was off on a gambling binge and having the last laugh again or Phillip was history, soon to be on his way to the cooling board. Don't waste a perfectly good prayer, I decided: He's either all right or he's dead. You should have prayed yesterday, my gal.

"Please pray for Phillip if you can," I asked my sister and everyone who telephoned me after they heard the news. I thought it might help Phillip on his astral journey — it was Yom Kippur the day they threw his remains into the ocean and I clung to the hope that prayers might help Phillip escape further torment in some way. Yes, I'm a hypocrite, all right, but not enough of one to pray for Phillip after kicking him into the grave.

But where was his grave? He had no grave any more than he had a body. "Now you see it; now you don't," Phillip used to say on stage during his tricks. He was there, his lustrous virile body turning its back to me and walking away, and then he was "gone." The old lady who lived next door to him identified the body for the coroner — no loved one ever saw Phillip again.

"We need a body," my sister said, but there wasn't one.

"But where's his grave?" Carlo asked. "Where's the thing with his name on it — the place you go with flowers?"

"There isn't one," I told my son. "They had him burned up and thrown out of an airplane."

"That isn't right," Carlo responded, correct as always, my little child.

I did thank God profusely for sparing Phillip that first time — the time he did or did not take a bottle of antidepressants and did live to kiss me thousands of times more. Now I thank Him for the fact that Phillip's "cremains" were thrown away like stinky chicken bones are tossed into the garbage can. Because loving a ghost is bad enough. Pressing my lips to Phillip's pillow and kissing it every night and crying is bad enough. At first, the pillowcase smelled of bleach and Phillip's hair and a trace of cigarette smoke, but now it smells of dust, and I kiss it still. "Phillip, my darling, I love you," I say, and I writhe a bit against the mattress and sometimes I tongue the pillow, which is dry and unyielding and makes a strange rasping sound as I kiss it.

Were there a grave to visit, I would not be just a ghost-lover, but I would be a ghoul as well. I would go there again and again, bearing armloads of flowers, just like the pale roses I threw into the ocean that day with Dr. Roth; and I would hurl myself onto Phillip's grave and do my crying there in the open, rather than in my spooky little bedroom. I would claw at the sod and earth, my fingernails growing black with dirt; I would bang on the coffin I never saw, that in fact never was. I would long for the waxen body, beginning to be food for the bugs, no longer feeding my desire. I would be a grave-defiler, a lover of the decaying, bonded to putrefaction. I would chain myself to his coffin until I too were on the other side.

But Phillip has no body, so he's the other kind of ghost: the kind like George Kirby in *Topper* or Joe in *Heaven Can Wait*. My body is the one that is rotting away — Phillip will always be a young man wearing a brown leather jacket, walking away with curls on the back of his head and lovely curving buttocks, moving down the walkway and out of sight.

reunion

There is no way to avoid them anymore, she thinks. If you run your errands in a nice part of town, there they are, swarming like fruit flies around the yuppies and landed gentry, sucking, sucking for nectar. But you find them in the lousy parts of town, too, because that's where they really live, even if they do call themselves "homeless." They rent cheap apartments there and roll out in the afternoon to begin begging, sometimes at the nearest fast-food outlet or in the parking lot of the video rental place, where there is always lots of foot traffic.

She thinks the worst ones are the guys who try to wash the windshield of her car—she really hates them. She can put up with the "Spare change?" guys, and the "Scuze me—scuze me!" guys who never get any further than that with her, because she wears dark glasses so they cannot see her eyes as she walks impassively by them. But the ones who pretend to hire themselves out as windshield-washers when they are actually aggressive panhandlers—they are the ones she cannot stand, because they are deceitful.

One of them sidles up to her in the parking lot of the video rental store, in the slimy ambling way some of them have, trying both to intimidate her and to appear pathetic at the same time, an art form. He begins to whine something but she cuts him off before he gets anything out. "No, thank you," she says and walks past him without a glance.

She realizes she has come full circle, because she is now just like her ex-husband. She had second thoughts about him on their honeymoon, and it was because of a windshield-wiping incident. The U.S. economy was still good then, so no one had ever tried to wash their car's windshield for cash at home. But the newlyweds had traveled south of the border and certain things were different. When they exited a dusty little café there were two small boys by their car, street urchins who had glommed on to the VW bug the couple had driven all the way to Baja. She and her husband were laughing when they came out of the café — they had been married only two days and were in a strange country which was nothing like Hawaii. He had traveled to third-world countries, but she had not. She was enjoying the culture shock from the unfamiliar language and customs and the exotic climate.

In the café, when they had asked for "Café, por favor," they were given cups of hot water and little packets of instant Nescafe with Spanish instructions printed on them. The clock on the wall was an hour faster than her groom's watch and they thought his watch must have broken. It had not occurred to them that they had entered a different time zone. There was something about the café that made it seem improvised, theatrical. The instant coffee and mismatched crockery reminded her of her childhood when she and her sister had played make-believe restaurant on the family patio, writing down each other's orders in their school notebooks and wearing their mother's aprons as costumes.

The waifs outside the cafe wiped their car's windshield vigorously and demanded dinero. When they stood insisting to her husband, "Feefty cenz," David glared at them and waved them away. Her stomach flipped over. It was midmorning and the boys were both under twelve years old and she thought they should be sitting at their desks in school. Instead they were out in the road pleading with tourists for a pittance. "They washed the windows, just give them the money," she told her husband.

He had not asked them to wash the windows, he reminded her. "Fifty cents — they're bandits in any case," he said.

"They're *children*," she said, but he got into the car with his jaw set hard and drove away from the youngsters.

And now, when she sees the scruffy men with the foraging eyes and the spray bottles ready to land on her car, she never thinks, The poor soul, but instead, Oh, that son-of-a-bitch, and steels herself against them. She thinks of how much she dislikes her job and how little money she has even for necessities, and she resents the panhandlers riding on the backs of those who work. She has become pragmatic.

"I can do the whole thing," the man in the parking lot insists, following after her with his spray bottle. She thinks she smells vomit. "The whole thing for just spare change." He is invading her personal space. She feels menaced, and she wants to turn around and get back into her car as quickly as possible and to drive brutally away from him. To run him down if she must. She would say, "Leave me alone," but she does not wish to be mistaken for a racist. He is probably looking at her leather handbag and her silk blouse and thinking she must be richer than her battered car might indicate. He cannot know that she buys nothing except at thrift shops or sales, that she is one-year's salary in debt.

He moves close to her car, so that he is nearly touching it and so that his body forms a bulwark between her and the video store and she has to swerve around him to get by. She knows they are both aware that he is large and male and that there are only the two of them in the lot. She makes the mistake of looking at him then, and he has a contrived, big dumb ingratiating look on his face, the foxy look of a con man. She knows con men, though, boy does she know them. Phillip had been a crash-course in con artists. He conned his way into her life when she was on the rebound from divorce, and though she spotted him from the start as an operator, he did manage to put one over on her now and then. He was irresistible in any case. The last time he fooled her, he bought a pair of new shoes, had an expensive haircut at Yosh, took her to dinner, then went home by himself and swallowed fifty Seconals like after-dinner mints.

"No, thank you," she repeats to the man with the spray bottle and tries to walk away from him, but he trots along beside her.

"How tough are those tires of yours?" he mutters, the jive-ass con-man look gone.

"You're vermin," she says, hardly believing the words have actually come from her. She feels a nervous euphoria and is just on the verge of breaking into a laugh. Once she had a neighbor who told her he had a heart attack on a bar stool, but that at the time he thought he had been stabbed. This is the polar opposite, because for an instant she feels a tug at her heart, a stinging heaviness and she gasps, thinking she is having a coronary. But then she feels him pushing against her, smells his dirty hair and feels his army jacket brush her cheek as he shoves her and goes on his way. She does not realize there was a knife until she sees the blood ruining her yellow silk blouse. She puts her hand to her side reflexively and it comes away wet crimson and she sees that the blouse is a goner. This is not much different from a menstrual acci-dent, really—just a nasty surprise, not even all that painful, just awk-ward. She walks toward the door of the video store, meaning to ask for help from a nice woman clerk. "Excuse me," she will say, "Excuse me, but I seem to be hemorrhaging." But first the sun grows searingly bright and she feels she will be flash-fried that very instant, like a pan-braised abalone. But the light goes out—pop!—like a bad light bulb, and the parking lot is immediately darkened. She has a revelation: The house lights are down, intermission is over. She feels herself sinking, but there is no impact as her knees crumple and she goes down, it is more like a wilting. This she knows already: This is the easy part. It's slipping into me, she thinks, just slipping into me so easily. It is like the first time you're with a new lover, and you thought it would be so difficult and you struggle and resist and then, just like warm silk you've slipped into each other. And she sees Phillip then, just as she knew she would, but it's not the way she wanted it to be, there is no merging, no contact. He is shining there, smiling, looking like the cover of the Sergeant Pepper album after she took acid, per-fectly bright and astonishing and welcoming and funny as hell.